Shifter

Spirian Saga Book 7

Rowena Portch

Shifter

AEON ENTERPRISES, INC., MARCH 2014

www.AeonEnt.com

Cover illustration and book design by
Aeon Enterprises, Inc.

ISBN — 978-0-9886275-5-0
Library of Congress Control Number: 2014905321
V1.0_r1

Printed in U.S.A.

ACKNOWLEDGMENTS

GREGG, you are a wonderful mate. Thank you for sticking with me through all my adventures in life. I know it's hard to be married to a female with a gypsy soul. God bless you, my angel. You are and always will be my best friend.

Tyler, my editor, thank you from the depths of my soul for your incredible editing talent. Like a true artist, you've made this story shine. What a Godsend you are.

Daughter, **Erika**. Your skill of storytelling inspires me to continue writing. I know your own novels will be a huge success. Thanks for your undying support and cheerful spirit. Most of all, thank you for my wonderful grandchildren who make me smile.

Nick, Andrew, and **Zach**, you are the most gifted sons a mother could ask for. Not only do you encourage me to continue pursuing my dreams, but you call when I need to hear the words, "I love you, Mim." Thank you.

To the females in my life, **Mum**, **Evelyn**, and **Georgian**, bless you for the girl time, the laughs, your support, and most of all, your unconditional love. I couldn't make it without you.

Cast of Characters

Khalen (Kay-len) — North America's regional leader of the Grandhun clan; Skye's mate; father to Kaili, Shaiya, Gabrihen, and Zhentu; reaper.

> **Skye** — Khalen's mate; mother to Kaili, Shaiya, Gabrihen, and Zhentu; legendary healer.

> **Kaili** (Ky-lee) — Eldest daughter of Khalen and Skye; animal communicator.

> **Shaiya** (Shy-ya) — Kaili's twin; healer.

> **Gabrihen** (Gay-bre-hen) — Khalen and Skye's eldest son; wizard.

> **Zhentu** (Zhen-tu) — Khalen and Skye's youngest son; wolf shifter.

Seth — Khalen's nephew; leader of the Uig clan; mated to Rae; Elle's templar; reaper.

Connor — Eldest son of Elle; guardian son of Drew; Gabrihen's closest friend; alchemist.

Shifter

Ian — Khalen's closest friend; Aidan's younger brother; mated to Arcadie's daughter, Erika; Sunjia's templar; illusionist.

Aidan — Ian's older brother; Khalen's closest friend; Skye's templar; mated to Sunjia; illusionist.

Arcadie (Ar-cay-dee) — Spirian Elder; mated to Kitta; Skye's uncle; eldest son of Shanuk; elementist.

Case — Khalen's guardian father; Spirian Elder; son of Shanuk, Arcadie's younger brother; mated to Eve; elementist.

Tetris — Gabrihen's teacher; Case's closest friend; third-generation wizard.

Tiban (Ti-ban) — Leader of the Northern territories; Zebastian's father; mated to Shinda; mountain lion shifter.

> **Shinda** — Tiban's mate; mother to Zebastian and deceased son, Carter; fox shifter.

> **Zebastian** — Eldest son of Tiban; wolf and panther shifter, and a reaper.

Ren — Elder; Shanuk's youngest brother; guardian father to Teak; eagle shifter.

> **Teak** — Son of Ren; Zebastian's closest friend; eagle and bear shifter.

Bennet — Shadow leader of North America; evil to the core; elementist.

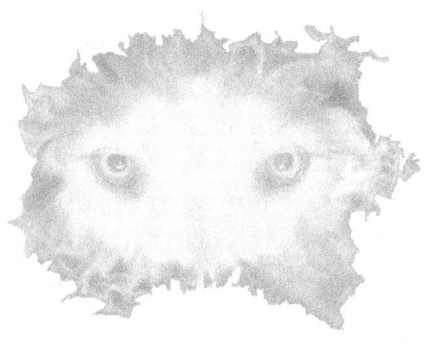

Prologue

~Kaili~

OVER FIVE YEARS HAVE PASSED since my brother, Zhentu, was abducted. He's the youngest of my siblings and a shifter.

Not much is known about shifters and why they are so different from other Spirians. It is believed that Fae blood is required to produce shifter offspring. Legend claims that when the first Angels descended from heaven to live as Spirians, they coupled with the Faeries, thus making the Spirian bloodlines strong and diverse in gifts.

Despite my attempt to learn more about shifters, their origin remains a mystery. Unlike typical Spirians, shifters have an animal spirit, making them wild and unpredictable at times. They are stronger than other Spirians, and often struggle to control their instinct to fight. Something about them fascinates me, but I can't say what intrigues me the most. When they shift into their animal form, I feel their thoughts as if they were my own as I do with any animal. It's my gift, though I'm not sure how useful it is.

Shifter

Zhentu's spirit was the wolf. Because shifters' have unique blood, they have gained the attention of the Shadows, dark Angels who seek to imbalance the scales that monitor good and evil.

Bennet Graves, is one such Shadow and a powerful leader who is not used to being thwarted. The rare female for whom he paid a lofty sum became the mate of my Uncle Seth. When Bennet had tried to take her back, my father, Khalen, defeated him in battle. This makes Bennet the prime suspect behind Zhentu's abduction. The Shadow remains recluse, however, and hasn't made any demands. Why?

Chapter 1

~Zebastian~

THE FURY IN MY FATHER'S gray eyes sparkled like demons threatening to break free to stab me in the heart. I had not seen him this angry since I was nine when my brother, Carter, and I wandered too far from camp and became lost. It took Father three weeks to track us down. Today, the anger resided deeper, visceral and unrelenting.

"You had one job, Zebastian: keep your brother safe. Now I discover that it was you who killed him—to save yourself?"

He paced before me, eyes narrowed, mouth held firm and straight—his pondering stance, a posture he took when making a tough but necessary decision.

"Your actions portray those of the Shadows, and are unforgivable."

"Father, I—"

As clan leader, he harnessed the ability to bind people in an energetic hold that could kill if necessary. The pain of it now gripped me like the claws of his shifter animal, the mountain lion. I couldn't breathe, let alone explain.

Even if I could explain, my father spoke truth. Carter lay dead, his blood still sharp in my throat. No longer able to hold myself up, I sank to the ground, grateful to land on the cold snow-covered surface.

When Carter and I escaped from the group of Shadows who took us twelve years past, the rage took over, darkening my soul to match that of our torturous captors. The only memory remaining was my brother's throat in my mouth, his copper-tasting blood coating my tongue.

"You have disappointed me, Zebastian. I was wrong about you." Father's energetic hold choked my air and constricted my organs, but hearing the words he spoke hurt like the lash of a soaked bull whip over and over as it tore through my soul, ripping the flesh of my pride.

My father meant everything to me. He had trained me to lead this clan since the time I could walk. Now, I had let him down, being every bit the monster he claimed me to be.

"I ban you from this clan, Zebastian. You are no longer—my son."

Death held mercy, but this—this was unbearable.

"No, Tiban!" Mother screamed. "You can't."

Ren, our clan elder, held her back. "Stay back, Shinda, leave him be for now." He was a man of stature in his own right, adoptive father of my closest friend, Teak.

The elder had led this clan for many years before relinquishing it to Father. Pain laced Ren's voice, yet he supported Father's decree, pulling my mother back, keeping her from reaching me. Red hair clung to her tear-soaked face as trembling hands reached toward me. Her image etched my memory; the last I would see of her—the last I would see of our home in Canada.

Father turned to step away, then hesitated to add, "You are Khalen's problem now. He will address your Shadow soul as he sees fit."

Father's regal, departing form blurred through my tears. My spirit wavered, teetering on the brink of desertion. I had been banished, removed from my clan. At twenty-four, I would not survive for long.

As Father so bluntly pointed out, I was Khalen Dunning's problem now. The regional leader of North America had a reputation—all bad if you were considered a Shadow. He made Father's wrath seem like a hand slap.

Teak reached down to lift me.

"Take him," Ren ordered. "Stay with him. Keep him safe."

Chapter 2

~Zebastian~

TEAK WAS NOT A SMALL man by any measure. His spirit animal represented the eagle: strong, regal, and swift. Like me, he had a secondary animal: the grizzly bear. His height of 6' 7" towered mine by a good four inches.

"I can walk," I groaned.

He carried me as if gliding over the ground. I floated in his arms, weightless as a breeze. Perhaps I was; perhaps I just imagined the lightness, the wind, and the cold.

"Don't talk. We're almost there."

We crossed the snow line and headed toward the trees that bordered Canada and Washington. The distance he managed was impossible, yet here we stood. Images faded in and out of my mind, blurring the barrier between illusion and reality.

MY EYES FLUTTERED OPEN, STRUGGLING against the need to sleep. I lay in a dark cave under furs by a fire. The scent of meat, broth, and sweet root vegetables permeated the air. Attempting to sit, I fought waves of nausea and dizziness clouding my mind.

"Teak, he's up," said a stranger's voice; it sounded male, young, with a hint of attitude.

I wanted to slap myself, force my wits to surface and function. Everything moved in slow motion. My hands felt numb, my limbs weak.

Teak entered the cave with a dripping bota bag in his hand. "You're awake."

"That's debatable. Where am I?"

Handing me the bota bag, he lent a hand to steady me. "Somewhere in the foothills of Bellingham."

I sipped the cold water, letting it awaken my body and senses with its clear mineral-rich purity. Never had water tasted so good as it did at this moment.

"How long have I been out?"

He sat cross-legged beside me. "Three days."

A young man peeked into the cave entrance, curiosity lacing his expression. Teak looked at him and shook his head. The man clenched his jaw and grumbled something as he closed the flimsy cover.

"What is this place, Teak? What's going on?" I asked.

"What do you remember?"

I took another long pull of the water, wanting something stronger; something to make me forget the memories that surfaced like hungry Gremlins.

"My inevitable death."

He chuckled as if I had said something amusing. "Yet, here you are, my friend, alive and well."

"And where is here, Teak? Who are those people outside?"

"Later," he said, tossing a twisted twig into the fire. "Right now, I'm more interested in what happened to you. Who took you? From where did you escape? What is SOAR?"

SOAR—those letters scorched my mind's eye like a brand of evil over my heart.

"I'm hungry. What is there to eat?"

Teak studied me as if trying to solve a mystery. "This is important, Ze. I'll come back with some food, and then you will talk to me, yes?"

I had never seen such intenseness in his near-black eyes. He had to be of Knik descent with his dark skin and chiseled features. He wasn't a ripped man in the sense of muscles and brawn. No, Teak was built more like a cheetah, all power and speed with strength that seemed to come from nowhere.

"Very well, my friend. We'll talk when you return."

I watched him stand with the grace of a subtle breeze, thinking about what I could tell him. So much of it was a blur in my mind.

I remembered growing weaker by the day, my spirit just a sliver of light, struggling against the heavy darkness of a cold hell.

I remembered cries echoing off the stone walls as howls of pain and despair clung to the dampness like moss on trees.

Teak returned with a bowl filled with steaming stew and flatbread. He handed them to me before setting down a bag in his hand and reaching for another log to add to the fire. When he was satisfied with the arrangement of emblazoned wood, he sat back down beside me.

The stew was spicy, hot, and thick with pepper, potatoes, and carrots. My stomach welcomed the hearty substance, grateful for having something to digest. The bread tasted dry but flavorful with herbs and seeds.

Teak stared into the flames, poking at the stray red embers that had scattered when he adjusted the wood. Patient as he appeared, he wouldn't wait for long to hear my story.

I took another swig of water before setting my half-eaten meal aside in hopes of having room for the rest later. I wondered who had prepared it. Teak could cook, but his idea of a meal involved meat skewered over an open flame.

"I searched for you," he said, "every day since the time you were taken."

The sip of water I tried to swallow struggled against my throat as if competing for space. I was twelve when taken; Teak lagged behind me by a year. The thought of him looking for me at such a young age appeared inconceivable, yet I believed him.

Teak had remained my constant companion since the day Ren brought him home, bundled in furs, almost dead. The elder asked me to care for him. I did the best I could.

"Talk to me, Ze. What happened that day?"

I took another long swallow, feeling the bite of a deep thirst that couldn't be quenched. "You were there, Teak. Why don't you tell me?"

He drew a deep breath, his jaw ticking like an overstretched string. "Very well. Twelve of us ventured into the woods that day. Your father tasked you with leading our first hunt. We shifted into our beast forms, you and your brother as wolves, me as my eagle. The others chose wild cats. The hunt was successful; we managed to bring down several moose, enough to feed the clan for months."

I picked at my food, trying to bring forth the memory of the events he spoke of. They were a haze, pieces of a mismatched puzzle in time.

"The first dart hit Carter. He went down hard. You ordered the others to scatter, to flee through the woods. You stayed behind, guarding your brother. There were five men with dart rifles. Two darts entered your side. I attacked the man who shot you, but another grabbed my wing and snapped it like a brittle twig."

My gut twisted with the thought as the sound of broken bones echoed in my mind, distant yet real all the same.

"I don't know how you did it, but you managed to bring down three of the men before they could find the others. I shifted back to my human form, in time to stop my attacker from sticking me with a needle. He was so strong, much too strong for me to battle. The needle poked through my skin, burning with the liquid it dispersed."

Flashes of his story played in my head, like broken film. "I couldn't save you."

"But you did, Ze. Don't you remember? You sprung out of nowhere, downing the man, distracting him from me. I was able to hide."

I remembered nothing.

"The other man hit you again with another dart. He made a comment about how it was sure to kill you. He grabbed Carter, while the other one dragged you away. I couldn't follow. I had no idea where they took you. I didn't even know if you were alive."

"There were times I wished I wasn't."

"Where did they take you?"

"I don't know. I woke up in a dark cell with no one around, including Carter. I couldn't shift back into human form. The walls were lined in lead."

Teak stiffened. Lead was the one substance that could

render Spirians giftless. "What was that like?"

"It felt hollow and empty, like life without any will."

He shuddered as if experiencing the coldness of it all. Spirians were born of the Angels; it was the Father's light that fueled our gifts, our powers. Without it, we were nothing but empty souls trapped in a human body.

"What did they want with you?"

"I don't know. They took my blood and injected me with some sort of serum."

"Testing you?"

"Perhaps, but why?"

"They're only taking shifter children," said Teak. "They have facilities all over the Northwest. The organization is called SOAR. I had hoped you knew what it stood for."

"They moved me around a lot," I replied. "I remained separated from other shifters until they sent me to Castlerock. My captors never spoke this word, 'SOAR.' They only bore it on their coats and shirts."

"Castlerock. Is that where you escaped from?"

"Yes, including Carter and many others. I built up a tolerance for the drugs they gave me, and could fake indisposition. I don't remember much after that."

Only the rhythmic sound of the crackling flames broke the heaviness of uncomfortable silence.

"And Carter?"

There it was, the elephant in the cave, so to speak; the crux of my failure.

"I killed him."

His dark eyes sparkled in the firelight, wide with shock and doubt. "I do not believe that, Ze. You wouldn't have done that—ever."

"Carter's throat was in my mouth, Teak. The only thing stopping me from ripping him apart was the voice in my head."

He looked as if he'd just swallowed a bug. "The voice?"

I stared into the flames. "Yeah, a female. She had the voice of an Angel."

Teak cleared his throat, no doubt stifling a derogatory comment. "What did this Angel say?"

"Stop!"

His lips pursed, making him look like a confused camel. "Ah, that does sound angelic."

I picked up a twig from the ground and tossed it into the flames. "You asked. I told you."

"Don't get your fur in a muddle, Ze. I'm just saying it sounds kind of weird, ya know?"

I gestured toward the cave's opening with a nod. "So who are they?"

"Your new clan."

"I have no clan, Teak, not anymore."

"Now you do."

I stood.

"Wait, Ze. These people need you."

"No, they don't. I am done leading, Teak. I don't want that responsibility. I just want to be left alone."

"Don't be stupid, Ze. Where are you going to go? How long will you survive without other Spirians?"

He leaned down to retrieve the bag he had brought in earlier with my meal. "At least clean yourself up. You look like the Wolfman having a bad hair day."

I caught the bag he tossed me.

"I'll wait for you outside."

In the bag, I found a mirror, brush, disposable razor, shaving cream, a fresh pair of jeans, and a black long-sleeved sweatshirt.

The mirror reflected how much had changed in the last

twelve years. A man, not a boy, stared back at me now. My jaw had squared out, my chest broadened. I still sported my mother's almond-shaped eyes and my grandfather's steel-gray irises with dark blue highlights. The years of pain and torture shone in the reflection staring back at me.

I had cut my hair before speaking to my father the day he cast me out. I had also shaved my face for the first time in too many years. My tribal roots blessed me with sparse facial hair, but the soft stubble of growth still cast a shadow over my face—a throwback from my mother's Irish blood, I was sure.

As I lathered my chin and jaws with shaving cream, I reveled in how much I mimicked my father in looks. We shared the same dark skin, jet-black hair, and lips that had a natural curl at the corners.

The clothes Teak had packed for me were excessively tight for my comfort, but they were clean and would do for now.

I stepped outside to see at least twenty or so young adults staring at me as if I had sprung horns from my head. I began walking past them when a comment stopped me short.

"I knew he would peter out," spoke a cocky young man.

I turned to face him. He stood daunting as a mountain—not so much tall as he was broad. He looked my age, about my height, and of Spanish descent. The thin mustache he sported gave him a punk-like appeal.

"I'm sorry; do I know you?"

"No, and by the looks of it, you never will."

"Yippee for me."

The punk bristled, moving toward me as if to invoke

a challenge. Was he kidding? Shifters were aggressive by nature, but prompting a fight over something so trivial proved excessive.

"Stop!" Teak ordered. "You don't want to do this, Bender. Ze will send you into next Sunday so fast you'll forget the past three days."

Bender spat at my feet. "He's a coward."

I felt the weight of everyone's eyes upon me, waiting to see my reaction. The real question was, did they really want to see it? My rage didn't have a good track record of ending things well.

"You want to lead this bunch?" I asked him. "Go ahead; be my guest." I pushed my way past his bulky frame.

He shifted into a grizzly bear and swiped at my leg, shredding my jeans. Blood seeped down my calf, soaking my leather shoes.

"Oh boy," Teak muttered as I shifted into my wolf. "Everyone, stand back."

Chapter 3

~ K a i l i ~

MY HEART SLAMMED IN MY chest as the vision grew clearer, taking my thoughts on an abandoned ride with no destination. The magnificent gray wolf with steel-gray eyes fought a uniformed man, trying to defend a smaller black wolf. The man had a knife. He intended to slit the black wolf's throat. "Stop!" My voiced echoed off the painted walls, snapping me out of my vision.

Everyone in class turned to face me. Our instructor, Mr. Hammond, stopped reading and slid his glasses down on his nose. The bald strip down the center of his head reflected the blue glow from the overhead lights.

"Is there something wrong, Miss Dunning?"

My mind had been elsewhere, somewhere dark and dismal. How long was the vision? What was Mr. Hammond reading?

"No—yes—I mean, I need to go." Grabbing my books and bag, I didn't wait for his reply. I had to find my twin, Shaiya, and tell her what happened. She would be in dance class this hour. The performing arts building stood halfway across campus.

I ran, stuffing my books into my bag as I hurried down the corridor. The wolf shifter I envisioned was connected to my baby brother, Zhentu; he had to be.

Five years ago, during a battle in Uig, Zhentu disappeared. Father had every Spirian on alert to find him. Since that day, many other young Spirians disappeared as well. Somehow, I knew the shifter male in my vision could help. Now I just had to find him.

I pushed the door and continued to run.

An older gentleman waved his hand. "Hey, slow down, missy. No running in the halls."

I ignored him, rushing past. Thank God it wasn't raining. A clear spring day in Washington was a rarity; then again, summer was just around the corner.

Turning left through the Red Square, I headed west toward Shaiya's building. She practiced in PAC room sixteen, I think she said.

Jazz music blared through the doors as a couple of females wandered out carrying bags and tape-wrapped dance shoes. They didn't spare me a second glance as I brushed past them.

Shaiya was dancing with a tall male, she called "The Rhino," on account that he resembled one when he danced. They argued now about the way Shaiya held her arms.

"I'm just saying," the Rhino quibbled, "you look like a flipping faery who lost her ability to fly."

"I am a faery, you dolt. Our performance is called Dance of the Faeries, remember?"

When her gaze fell on me, she didn't hesitate. She turned her back on Rhino and came toward me, her sweet, heart-shaped face scrunched in concern.

The Rhino cursed under his breath. "Hey, where are you going? We have to work on this, Shaiya. Our performance is next month, remember?"

She held up her hand. "I remember. Give me a moment, will ya?" Her green eyes studied mine. They were a shade paler than mine but far more intense. "Hey, are you okay? You look like you've seen a ghost."

"Shaiya, I saw him. He can help find Zhentu, I know it."

She brushed a blonde strand of hair from my dampened face. "Who did you see?"

"That wolf shifter. The one in my dreams."

She smiled, looking hopeful. "You mean the hot one who looks like a black-haired Jason Stratham on steroids?"

I rolled my eyes at the image she conjured based on my dream. "Yes, that one." The man was more rustic than Jason, but I wasn't going to bring that up.

Shaiya looked around at the audience who showed more interest in our conversation than was necessary. "Come with me."

I followed her out of the room and down the hall. We slipped into an empty room that looked like a storeroom for broken speakers and such.

Unlike me, Shaiya wore her hair short and somewhat spiky. Mine was long, past my waist; not quite as thick as Mum's, but it was just as blonde with white streaks running through it. Shaiya and I were the same height, but she was thinner and far more graceful than I could ever dream of being. She had athletic abilities, where I was blessed with intellect, or so I was told.

Shaiya cleared off two chairs. "Sit; tell me what happened."

I could always count on my twin to listen without

judgment.

"This shifter, I'm connected to him. I feel him and hear his thoughts—his shifter thoughts."

"Not so strange considering you talk to animals."

"I've never met this man."

She smiled, sitting back in her chair. "From what you told me of your dreams, I'd say you know him very well."

Heat flooded my face. "Yeah, well, we both know those dreams were based on fantasy, yes?"

"There's a thin barrier between fantasy and reality, dear sister. Besides, your fantasy was way better than any reality I've experienced."

I huffed. "At least you have experience."

"You would too if you weren't so bloody picky."

"I haven't found anyone I like."

"Thomas is sweet on you. Why don't you date him?"

The image of Thomas, a short, skinny guy in my chemistry class, made me shiver. He was nice enough, and had a great personality, but he was just too—sweet. "No, I don't think so."

"Let me guess. You don't like 'nice guys.'"

"I like them, I'm just not ... attracted to them."

"Whatever. Tell me about your vision."

"Well, my wolf broke out of this dark mansion-like place, with about seven shifters."

"Your wolf?"

"The man in my vision. Anyway, they fought so many Shadows; it was like watching a massacre. Then, there was this black wolf. My wolf seemed connected to him. During the fight, the Shadow did something horrible. I told him to stop but he didn't hear me. My wolf shifter hesitated. I think he heard me."

"Did he stop the Shadow?"

I thought for a moment. "I don't know. Everything happened so fast. The Shadow rolled over, pulling the black wolf with him. There was so much blood."

"Wow." Shaiya pressed her face into her hands. "Man, I don't want your visions. They sound horrid."

"I think this shifter can help find Zhentu."

"Maybe. Let Father know."

I pulled at a loose string on my shirt. Telling Father might not be the best idea. "I was kind of thinking you and I could find this shifter."

"Oh, no. That is not a good idea, Kaili. Father told us to stay on campus—period. In case you haven't heard, children are missing from around here."

"I'm not a child anymore, and neither are you. I need to find this guy, Shaiya. He's the key to finding Zhentu. I know it."

"Then let Father know. He will find your man. He, Mum, and Gabrihen are coming tonight. You can tell them at dinner, yes?"

Her words made sense, and if Father discovered we went in search of this shifter alone without his knowledge, we would lose our freedom for quite some time. "Very well."

DINNER WITH MY FAMILY ALWAYS proved intense. Mum behaved as if she would never see us again, Father gave his typical lecture about staying on campus, and Gabrihen, our younger brother, acted as if he were already in charge. Granted, Father would deem him our leader when he was of age, but sometimes Gabrihen took things too far. He was two years our junior with a cockiness that stung like a thorn in my side.

Being the daughter of Khalen Dunning, the regional

leader, was no picnic. Being the daughter of the infamous legend, Skye Dunning, was even worse. For this reason alone, Shaiya and I chose Western University over the many ivy-league schools in Europe.

Somehow, when your parents were all that and a bag of chips, people expected things from you. Shaiya and I just wanted to be—normal.

Father ordered a few bottles of Borolo wine and three appetizers. The place was nice. Father had a thing for eating at fine restaurants, no matter the cost. Our bill would be close to $600 by evening's end, I was sure.

He poured my mum's glass first, before pouring one for my twin and me. His and Gabrihen's were filled last. He never paid much attention to the age limit for alcohol, seeing Spirians were immune to it unlike humans. To Father, eating a meal without wine was pure blasphemy.

He didn't have to worry too much about us being carded because he could manipulate the human mind as easily as one could change a radio station.

He raised his glass in salute. "Nice to have everyone together again."

We clinked our glasses, and then waited for Mum and Father's inevitable, often embarrassing, kiss before drinking. They still acted like newlyweds. It was awkward, yet comforting all the same.

The conversation stayed light for the most part. I noticed my mum had brought her sight cane, instead of Maiyun, her guide dog.

"How's Maiyun?" I asked.

Her shoulders dropped. "Tired."

"Mum, she's twenty-six years old. That's longer than most dogs live."

She stiffened and Father shook his head, warning me

to drop the subject.

"Kaili has some interesting news," Shaiya stated.

"You finally got laid?" Gabrihen asked.

That earned him a warning look from Father and Mum.

"Very funny, Gabe."

"Don't call me that."

"Enough," Father warned, in that tone that nobody challenged.

"What's your news?" asked Mum.

I told them about my dreams—well, most of them, anyway, and about the vision I'd had during class.

"And you think this shifter knows how to find Zhentu?" asked Father.

"I do. We are connected somehow, and I think it comes from Zhentu. It's the only thing that makes sense."

Shaiya chuckled. "Well, not the only thing."

I narrowed my eyes at her, which made Father smile. He had obviously tapped her mind. Gabrihen smiled as well. Mum had the decency to stay out of my business.

"Nice," I said. "Thanks," I mouthed to Shaiya.

She smiled in return—traitor.

"I'd like to try to find this man," I said.

The weight of Father's stare matched Gabrihen's. "No," they said together.

"Father, I'm no—"

He raised his hand. "Kaili. It took everything I had to allow you and your sister to come to this school. Do not make me regret that decision."

"Are you crazy?" Gabrihen hissed over the table. "Don't you get it? Shadows are taking Spirian children all over the northern territories. Do you want to add to their numbers?"

"I'm not a child, Gabrihen. I'm older than you."

"You're an unmated female."

"Stop it," Mum said. Though her voice was calm, all of us could sense the storm of her wrath in the distance. "I will not listen to you two bicker during our meal. Please, show respect for one another."

"Yes, Mum," I said. "Sorry."

"Sorry," Gabrihen muttered.

The evening progressed with lighter conversation; the subject of my vision long forgotten. That's what I thought, anyway. Father must have tapped my thoughts on the matter.

"I may know the young man in your vision."

That earned everyone's attention.

"Tiban Carue has a son. Rumor has it he killed his brother and was banned from the clan. His father claims he's dangerous and unpredictable."

A chill ran up my spine as I remembered the aggression the young man displayed. Had he turned? Was he a Shadow now?

"I think it's time I find this young man," said Father.

My appetite faded, as did my hope for the poor man who invaded my dreams. I silently prayed he had information to offer my father—something useful. Perhaps then, his life would be spared.

Chapter 4

-Zebastian-

BENDER CIRCLED ME, LOOKING FOR a weakness. He wouldn't find one and once he made his move this fight would be over. My leg throbbed as it continued to bleed. It only served to fuel my rage, something I struggled to keep controlled.

As our energy amped up, everyone took several steps back. Coming between a Spirian battle was dangerous; coming between two shifters was suicidal.

Bender saw an opening and made his move, baring large teeth and claws that made Freddie Krueger look like a kitten. Perhaps shifting to my panther form would have been more appropriate?

I dodged his attack, countering it with a bite to his leg, tearing his Achilles tendon. When he swiped at my chest, ripping it open, my rage kicked in—too strong to hold back now.

"Get back," I heard Teak say. It was the last thing I remembered.

Shifter

- K h a l e n -

I FELT THE PULSE OF Spirian energy, amping as if a war had begun.

"Do you feel that?" Gabrihen asked.

I nodded. "Can you track it?"

He had the ability to hone in on an energetic source, a gift reserved for wizards, or so I was told. Tetris, the mentor I chose for him, was a third-generation wizard. He had taught my son well over the past few years; his skills were strong.

"Yes."

"Take me there."

Transporting was also a gift reserved for wizards, though it was a difficult one to master. Gabrihen's lack of skill in that area made the journey a painful one.

"Are you sure?"

"I'm sure. Just concentrate this time, yes?"

Lips firm and eyes closed, he gripped my arm and poof, we were gone. It amazed me how powerful my son had become. At only eighteen, he showed promising leadership skills and courage that rivaled most elders.

We transported into the middle of a battle between a grizzly bear and a wolf—Spirian shifters. I dodged a blow from the bear just in time, and waylaid the wolf's bite. Gabrihen wasn't so lucky. He lay on the ground with the wind knocked out of him.

I helped him up. "Next time, try to get close to the energetic source, not bloody on top of it."

"Yeah, good idea."

The wolf with bright eyes, wild as winter, took the bear down in quick order before turning on me, lips pulled back in a snarl.

He leapt. I stepped aside, pounding my fist against the side of his neck. He came after me again, and then just stopped, looking confused.

I waited as he shifted back into human form. A taller man tossed a pair of jeans at him. Everyone else stood back, wide-eyed and quiet.

The bear, too, shifted back to human. He was in bad shape and would need Skye's help.

"Get your mum," I told Gabrihen. He nodded and then transported back to our cabin.

I looked at the young crowd gathered around me. I didn't remember a clan being here, or even close to here for that matter.

I looked at the wolf shifter with steel-gray eyes. "What is your name?"

He donned the pants the tall man had tossed him. With confidence, he looked me straight in the eye. "Have you come to kill me?"

I frowned. "Have you given me reason to?"

He bent down to retrieve a shirt that was now tattered. Shaking his head, he tossed it back to the ground. The wound on his chest seeped with blood, but it wasn't too deep. He was scared; I could see it, yet his scent didn't match the emotion. He smelled of rage and fury, not fear.

"You are Khalen Dunning," he said, "regional leader of the Grandhun clan."

"Aye, I am. And you are?"

"Zebastian Carue, son of—ex-son of Tiban, leader of the Tanuk clan."

I gestured to the man still lying on the ground. "And the man you tried to kill?"

"If I wanted to kill him, he'd be dead."

I liked this young man; he had spunk, courage, and an

attitude that needed some trimming. A bit rough around the edges, but no Shadow as Tiban had indicated.

"Your father informed me about you."

"No doubt."

"Is this your clan?"

"Yes," the tall man answered.

"No," said Zebastian, "it is not."

I looked back at the taller man, the one who had tossed Zebastian the pants. "Your name?"

He stepped closer to me, matching my stare with dark curiosity and confidence that matched Zebastian's. "Teak Lazatundrum, son of the elder, Ren."

Gabrihen returned with Skye. She fell to her knees and immediately purged her stomach.

"Rough ride?" I asked.

"I may have rushed things a bit," said Gabrihen.

Skye coughed a few times and then wiped her mouth. "I'm fine. Just a bit dizzy is all."

"If you clear the energetic path before transporting, you can avoid this," Zebastian said.

Gabrihen stood taller and met his eyes. "And what, pray tell, do you know about transporting?"

"My grandfather was a wizard."

"That doesn't make you an expert."

Zebastian shrugged. "Just thought you'd like to know." He glanced down at the young bear shifter on the ground, and then back to Teak. "What happened?"

That got my attention. He didn't know?

"He challenged you, and you accepted with your usual grace."

Zebastian noticed the gaping wound on my chest. "Did you get in the middle of it?"

The man was clearly confused. He wasn't faking it,

not according to his intentions, anyway. If he lied, I would have sensed it. "What do you remember, Zebastian?"

He gestured to the man on the ground. "Bender ripping open my chest."

"And that is all?"

"Not quite. The voice—the one that brought me back—I remember that."

"The voice?"

"His Angel," said Teak. "She ends his rage."

Skye finished healing the man called Bender before tending to Gabrihen and me.

"What did she say to you?" I asked.

"Stop!"

Gabrihen laughed. "Believe me, she's no Angel."

My mate gave her son a harsh look before healing Zebastian's wounds.

"Thank you," he told her.

She smiled up at him. "You're welcome." After a moment's hesitation, she added, "I can see what she likes in you."

"You know this woman who speaks to me?"

"She's our daughter," I explained.

Zebastian stood quiet for a moment. "Why does she speak to me?"

"She claims you are connected in some way. She believes you know where Zhentu is."

"Zhentu?"

"Our son," Skye explained. "He was taken five years ago. He's a shifter as well; a wolf like you."

"I don't know him."

"She believes you do."

"Then she's mistaken."

"She's crazy sometimes," said Gabrihen, "but she's

rarely mistaken when it comes to her visions."

"What's her name?"

"Kaili."

Zebastian looked lost, confused, and ready to bolt.

"Was Zhentu taken by the SOAR group?" Teak asked.

The name was not familiar to me. "SOAR?"

"It's the group that took Ze and these others."

I wrapped my arm around my mate's shivering body. "Is there somewhere warmer we can talk?"

"Come," said, Teak. "There's a fire burning in the cave."

Everyone followed except Zebastian.

"Are you coming?" I asked.

"If you're not here to kill me, I'd rather be on my way."

"On your way where?"

"I don't know yet."

"You're just going to wander about the woods alone?"

"That's the plan."

"Well, you will have to put it on hold for now until I find out what's going on."

"Teak knows more than I do. Talk to him."

"Zebastian, I'm not asking you; I'm telling you."

He stiffened and studied me for a brief moment before heading toward the cave. This man was spirited, but he was no Shadow. Of that, I was certain.

Chapter 5

~ K a i l i ~

IT WAS COMMON FOR SPIRIANS to have visions. Mine, however, were accurate to the point of being scary. Unlike my father who saw things before they happened, I saw things as they happened, as if looking through the eyes of another. Having visions about a man I never knew was new for me, and perhaps a bit frightening.

The man, himself, intrigued me. Was he a Shadow? If so, what was my connection to him, and why did he draw my attention?

Another vision had come to me earlier this morning while I studied. In his wolf form, my shifter fought a bear. Then, he went after my father. When Father's energy amped up, things often ended poorly for the one in his radar. The wolf charged for my father's throat. I yelled, "Stop!" just as I did before. The wolf seemed to snap out of some sort of trance. After that, the vision ended. I wanted to be there with my father and brother. I could help with this. Why wouldn't they let me?

A knock sounded upon my door. "Kaili?"

"Come in."

My sister poked her head through before stepping in with two steaming cups of joe in her hands. "I thought you could use some mo-joe." That's what she called my one-pump mocha.

"Actually, that sounds perfect right now." I took the cup from her hand. The scent of cinnamon and cocoa wafted up, blending nicely with the bitter bite of strong coffee. "Mmm." I took a sip. "Ahhh—why does the first sip of coffee in the morning always taste so good?"

Shaiya giggled and sat beside me on the bed. "I'm not sure, but it always does for me as well." She leaned forward, a gleam of excitement in her frosty-green eyes. "So, any more dreams?"

"No, but I did have another vision."

"And..."

"Father found the man; his wolf tried to kill Father; I stopped him."

She sat back, looking as if someone had taken her candy. "That's it?"

"Well, in a nutshell."

"Nutshell? I didn't ask for a nutshell; I want the juicy stuff, Kaili; come on."

I sent her my vision telepathically, seeing it would save us both quite a bit of time.

"Wow," she said, sitting back against the wall. How she did so without spilling her coffee astounded me. Then again, she was a dancer, graceful without limits, I suppose.

"What do you think Father will do to him?"

"Not my concern."

Her eyes widened. "Not your concern? Are you kidding me? We're talking about your children's father here and you're not concerned?"

I laughed. "My children's father, huh? I'm not so sure about that."

"Well, if Gabrihen has a say in it, the poor man won't be anyone's father."

Our little brother's idea of controlling the population of undesirables was to keep them from breeding. Lord, I hoped he wasn't serious.

I sipped my coffee and stared out the window at the misty rain. Everything looked gray and dismal outside. It almost made me grateful I had homework to do.

"Hey, wanna head down to the library for a bit?" asked Shaiya.

That got my attention. "You want to go to the library?"

"Yeah, I have studying to do as well, ya know."

I doubted it. Shaiya was one of those who never needed to study. She, too, had a photographic memory and an intellect that made mine look juvenile.

"Like what?"

"Okay, fine. There's someone I want you to meet. His name is Steed. He's an illusionist."

"Not interested, Shaiya."

"He's cute, tall, and built like a truck. Dark hair, blue eyes; what's not to like?"

"He probably thinks I look like you, act like you, and mirror you in every respect."

"No, not this time. He's actually in your biology class."

I would have noticed someone like him in my biology class. In fact, he would have stuck out like marble in a bed of glass. "I'm sure you're mistaken, dear sister."

"Come on. Just meet him."

"Ugh. Fine!"

Not only did Shaiya pick out my clothes, she went so far as to loan me a neon-pink blouse that she swore would bring out my eyes. Then, she insisted on braiding my hair. I looked like something out of *The Princess Bride*.

The library sat empty, as it typically did on a Friday afternoon. Most students were preparing for the weekend, not necessarily studying. If exams were coming up, it would be a different story.

Shaiya led me to the back room. A young man stood leaning against a bookshelf, reading a copy of *The Dao Te Ching*; not exactly a bad impression.

"Steed," Shaiya squealed. "Odd, seeing you here."

I gave her the look. Did this man not know we were meeting today?

Steed's liquid blue eyes looked me up and down as if enjoying a rare painting. "Hello."

Shaiya made a gesture that resembled something Vanna White would do on *Wheel of Fortune*. "Steed, this is Kaili, my twin." She then turned to me, making the same silly gesture. "Kaili, this is Steed."

The man smiled like a tiger trapping a tasty rabbit. Only, I was no rabbit.

He took my hand and kissed the back of it. "It is a pleasure to finally meet you."

I pulled my hand away. "Funny, I don't remember seeing you in my class."

He changed to a nerdy-looking freshman with pocked skin and thick glasses. He completed the image with a plaid, button-up shirt, and a pair of Dockers. His hair was brown, mussed, and his eyes lacked the incredible blue he had just moments before.

"Right," I said, "an illusionist."

He changed back to his handsome form, making me wonder what the man truly looked like.

"I can't stick around for long," he said. "I'm heading

to The White Stag later to meet some friends. Would you and Shaiya like to join us?"

The White Stag was a local club owned by our Father's friend, Jacob. It was a place where Spirians could mingle. Few humans knew of the place because it was hidden from them by what Jacob called "chimera"—an illusion of sorts.

"We'd love to come," Shaiya blurted out. "They have great dancing there and it's karaoke night."

"Father won't approve," I told her.

"It's Jacob's place. What could happen there?"

I turned to Steed. "I guess we'll see you there."

"Great. Seven o'clock?"

I nodded and watched him leave. The man could fill out blue jeans, that was certain. Him being an illusionist, though, was a concern.

"Now what?" asked Shaiya. "You have that look."

"What look?"

"The one that says, he's nice, but…"

"He's an illusionist, Shaiya. How do you know that what we're seeing is real?"

"Uncle Ian and Aidan are illusionists, and they're real."

"They're also dangerous."

She rolled her eyes. "Criminy, Kaili, can't we just go out and have a good time without you overanalyzing everything?"

"I'm just saying, we know nothing about this guy."

"I'm not asking you to bond with him, just go out and have fun."

Men our age always wanted one thing, a chance to mate without commitment. Spirians in their twenties were expected to experiment as much as possible so they would know what their true mate would look and feel like when it came time to join with him or her. Unlike human marriages, Spirians mated for life, so you had one chance to find the right partner.

Shaiya had plenty of experience already; she seemed to go through men as a child goes through candy. I, on the other hand, was still innocent. For a time there, Shaiya believed I was gay. It wasn't that; I just hadn't found anyone who kept my interest for more than a few moments. My looks seemed to attract the "nice guys." Those so called "nice guys" always ended up squashed under my steamroller personality. I didn't mean to be harsh; I just ended up that way. Timid and shy men tended to bring out the worst in me. Steed, on the other hand, was not timid or shy. In fact, he seemed a bit too confident for my comfort, making me wonder what he was truly up to.

Chapter 6

~Zebastian~

"I TOLD YOU, I KNOW nothing," I repeated.

Gabrihen looked at me with golden eyes that reflected the fire like solar orbs. He was the spitting image of his father, and looked to be far more mature than his mere eighteen years suggested. "My sister says you are connected to Zhentu."

"I told you she's mistaken."

"And I told you, she's never mistaken, not about stuff like this."

I had described my escape, and the woman's voice that had calmed my blinding rage. This young buck seemed to think it was the voice of his sister.

Teak tossed me one of his shirts. "You said you heard her again, when you were about to attack Khalen."

I squeezed into the shirt that was a size too small. "Yes."

"Tell me more about this SOAR group," said Khalen, apparently indifferent about his daughter's involvement.

I shook my head, fighting the memories that flooded

my mind with every question they asked me. I had tried so hard to forget the torture and pain, and here they were, dragging it all back to the surface.

"They kept us in cells," I said. "The walls were lined with lead to keep us from using our gifts. We were drugged most of the time, unless they were trying to invoke our anger."

"Invoke your anger?" asked Khalen.

"Yes, they prodded us with taser sticks, they kicked us, struck us with whips, chains, and anything else they had in hand to see how we would react."

"In time, I became immune to their abuse, and the drugs they continuously gave me."

"You said they gave you serum, yes?"

"Yes, it stung like hell. I think it made us more violent."

"That explains why they invoked your anger," said Skye. "They were testing you."

She was a quiet beauty with silver eyes. It was obvious she was blind, but she moved around with grace and seemed to require little assistance. Her blonde hair fell past her waist, even though she wore it in a braid.

Something about her eyes, however, haunted me. I had seen eyes like hers before, but where?

"You remember something?" asked Khalen, having read my thoughts.

"Fragments, but nothing solid."

"We need to get inside these facilities," said Gabrihen.

"No, that is impossible," I said. "They are heavily guarded. The dart guns they use can be deadly."

"How many facilities are there?" asked Khalen.

"I was taken to at least seven, that I remember. All of them here in the Northern territory."

Teak added another log to the fire. "They transport

the shifters in armored trucks, usually at night."

"Who is in charge of this SOAR group?" asked Khalen.

All eyes turned to me. "I don't know. Names were not spoken."

Khalen pointed to my chest area. "What happened there?"

I reached up and touched the sagging dip in my flesh. "They chipped us. I tore mine out."

Skye placed her hand over her belly as if fighting a wave of nausea. "Oh, God," she whispered. "Zhentu."

My heart went out to the woman, and I wondered whether my mother had felt the same when I had gone missing. Did she miss me now? Did Father?

Khalen gestured to the band of young teens meandering beyond the cave. "Tell me about these people. Where did they come from?"

Teak sat cross-legged beside me. "Bender and I rescued them from this SOAR group as they were being transferred. That is the only time they are not heavily guarded—until recently. Now they place guards in the trucks, making it difficult to get inside."

Khalen looked to me. "What was the fight between you and Bender about?"

"I made a mistake," said Teak. "I told the mob that Ze would lead them out of here. Ze had other plans. Bender called him a coward, and the fight began."

Khalen continued to stare at me quietly for a moment. "I see."

"Are we done here?" I asked, starting to stand.

"No," said Gabrihen. "You need to help us find Zhentu."

"I can't. I don't know where he is."

He looked between his mother and me. Then, his

expression changed as if he'd been struck with an epiphany. "Kaili feels the connection between you and our brother. She can help you remember."

Skye looked hopeful. "Yes, I think that will work."

"Take him to see her," said Khalen, without even asking my permission. "I will take care of this lot and meet you back at the cabin, yes?"

"Yes, Father."

"No." All eyes turned to me. "Sorry, but I have other plans."

Khalen's eyes glowed gold and I felt the hum of his energy amping. Taking him on would be a mistake, a fatal one I was sure.

"Your plans can wait, Zebastian. Right now, the only thing you need to do is help us find Zhentu and bring this organization down. After that, you are free to do as you wish."

Teak stepped between Khalen and me, absorbing the leader's stinging energy. "Please, Ze. We need to stop this SOAR group, whoever they are. What they did to you and these others is unspeakable. We could use your help."

Teak never pleaded for anything, but he was doing so now. Why was this so important to him?

"You know what happened to the others I tried to save," I replied.

Khalen pulled back his energy, allowing Teak to relax.

"Being a leader does not mean you never fail, my friend. It means you give everything you have to ensure your clan's safety."

"What I have is not enough."

He gestured back at Khalen. "You told me once you looked up to this leader. Now, you have a chance to help him and you turn your back?"

"What if I fail him?"

"At least you tried." His black eyes studied me. "I plan to help them. I need you there by my side."

"You don't know what you're getting into."

"But you do, and we could use that knowledge."

I groaned, thinking about how I had spent years trying to escape that place only to face it once again. They were asking me to break back in.

Khalen stepped toward me. "Your father tells me you've joined the Shadows, son. I don't share his opinion. Help me prove him wrong."

"How do you know he is wrong?"

"Let's just say I have a strong intuition."

I followed Gabrihen outside as he pulled an iPhone from his pocket. He dialed, waited, then cursed as the thing went to voicemail. "Damn it, Kaili; why don't you ever answer your phone?" He followed the call with another.

Two rings, three. "Hello?"

Having the heightened senses of my wolf was a real convenience at times like these.

"Shaiya, where's Kaili?"

"Hello, Gabrihen. Yes, it's nice to hear your voice as well."

"Cut the crap, Shaiya. Where's Kaili?"

"In class, why?"

"We found Zebastian, the man she envisioned. I need her help."

"She won't be back until after six. We're meeting some men at The White Stag if you want to join us there."

"Too noisy."

"Too bad," she said. "That's where we'll be."

"Fine, what time?"

"Seven." Silence followed. "Gabrihen?"

"Yeah?"

"This is the first time I got Kaili to meet a man, so please don't screw it up, okay?"

"She won't need my help in that department."

"I'm not telling her you're coming."

"Whatever." He ended the call and slipped the phone back into his pocket. "This will be fun."

Chapter 7

~Zebastian~

WHAT THE HELL WAS **I** thinking? Dematerializing was far worse than I remembered. Grandfather made it seem so easy. This young bloke, Gabrihen, still had much to learn.

If I could just help them find Zhentu, I would be free, released from Khalen's charge. I had been through worse, I assured myself.

"You all right?" Gabrihen asked. Somehow, the grin on his face didn't back his concern.

"Great," I groaned, still trying to peel my guts away from my spine. "Smooth transition."

"I took your advice and cleared the energetic path first."

Clearly he was still miffed over the advice I had given him earlier. He hadn't cleared the path first; he had dove head on into it like a bull in a china shop.

After purging my stomach in the bushes for the third time, I turned to face him, matching his sarcasm. "Glad I could help."

"Oh, yeah, it worked just fine."

Now he was just being cocky. When he stepped toward me wearing that shit-eating grin, my control eased away and my fist grew taut.

"You look a little green, Zebastian."

That did it. My fist connected with his mouth. He stumbled back, eyes glowing gold with rage. For a moment, he looked like he wanted to continue the fight, but then he raised his hands in surrender. "Okay, I may have deserved that one. We're even now, yes?"

Smart man. "Yes."

He rubbed his jaw and wiped a smear of blood from his lower lip. "Nice punch. You're fast."

"Let's hope you never have to find out how fast, boy."

"Boy? I'm scarcely younger than you."

I scoffed. "I doubt that."

"Age doesn't define a man."

"Something your father said?"

"Yes, and it's something I happen to believe."

I studied his golden eyes for a moment, seeing the man he wanted to be. I remembered being that young at one point, and knew the importance of shedding the youthful skin. I wanted people to see me for the man I thought I was, despite my age. I nodded to him.

"Ready to meet my sister?"

"You make her sound like a monster."

He laughed.

As we approached The White Stag, a line was forming on the outside. A huge red sign flashed, "21 and older." Gabrihen seemed to ignore the warning and marched to the front of the line.

"Samuel, how's it going tonight?"

The dark man smiled down at Gabrihen, who stood

an impressive inch taller than me. "Young Gabrihen, what brings you to this neck of the woods?"

"Business with my sister."

Samuel laughed. "Sounds serious. I'd best let you in then." He turned to open the door, giving me a look that assured me he would protect Gabrihen and his family, with everything he had if necessary.

Gabrihen called over his shoulder. "Want something to drink?"

"Yes."

The place was dark, loud, and crowded with Spirians. The bar sported a long curved burl wood counter with simple round stools covered in black leather.

Remnants of the old West clung to the walls like ghosts from a wild past. Peanut shells littered a distressed-wood floor and the place smelled of beer, spicy foods, and cheap cologne.

Gabrihen took a seat at the bar and ordered himself a Mac and Jack. The bartender looked to me next, a burly man with a scruffy beard and dark features that gave him a sinister look.

"What'll you have?"

"Water."

Ignoring the disapproving looks from both the bartender and Gabrihen, I focused on the female approaching the stage. Her short dress and poofy brown hair made her look like an '80s throwback.

"Next up, we have K—ylee, singing *Bitch* by Meredith Brooks."

"Man, she butchered that one," said Gabrihen, no doubt talking about the name.

I wasn't paying attention to the name or the woman speaking it. My attention was on the blonde waiting in the wings, young, innocent-looking—too bad for that. Her skin-tight jeans accentuated all the right places while her bright pink shirt made her green eyes shine like emeralds. A round of unenthusiastic applause preceded her entrance.

The song began to play and the woman belted it out like she wrote the thing. She had a voice, I'd give her that. The attitude with which she sang those enticing words made me wonder just how innocent she was. This evening still may have one redeeming factor, I hoped.

Gabrihen paid for his drink and then spun around to face the woman on stage. "She's good, yeah?"

"Very good. It's hard to picture someone like that singing those lyrics, though."

Gabrihen laughed. He had an odd sense of humor.

I picked up my glass of water and sipped it slowly, enjoying the minerals and coolness of it sliding down my throat.

"Sure you don't want something stronger?"

"Am I going to need it?"

"Most certainly."

I pictured his sister as a large, fanged woman with black hair and eyes the color of rubies. Could she really be that bad?

I turned to the bartender. "Black Bush." He nodded.

The woman on stage finished her song, exiting with a roaring applause from the crowd.

"Ready?" Gabrihen asked.

I grabbed my drink that he paid for, and then followed him toward the back of the club.

The young blonde who had sung the song was approached by a man. His confidence and assertiveness indicated he knew her. Her cold reaction to him, however, said the relationship was only one way.

"I liked the song," he said, pressing her against the brick wall. Apparently, the lyrics had the same effect on him as they did on me. Still, I didn't like the way he had her trapped. I started toward them, but Gabrihen held me back. "Wait," he warned.

The man pressed his hips against the blonde's. "How much of that song is true?"

"If you don't step back, Steed, you'll find out firsthand."

The gathering crowd started pushing back away from the couple, no doubt sensing the upcoming fray, or perhaps they noticed the bouncer making his way through the throng.

"I like a woman with spunk," Steed said, pressing her closer to the wall.

"Be easy on him, sister," another blonde announced.

When Steed captured her wrists and pinned them over her head, the tiny bit of goods stomped down on his foot, kneed his groin, and then pushed him back by his throat. He fell gasping on the ground until the bouncer grabbed him and hauled him away.

"Wow," I said, stunned at how easy she had made that look. "I wouldn't want to meet her in a dark alley."

Again, Gabrihen laughed at something that wasn't humorous.

The female joined another female with shorter, spiked hair. The two of them looked very similar if not identical.

"Come on," said Gabrihen. "Let's meet my sisters."

I followed him to the table where the young blonde had sat—not too scary looking. When her beautiful green eyes met Gabrihen's, they smoldered.

"Hello, brother," she drawled as if choking on sarcasm.

"Kaili, so nice to see you."

Judging by the venom in his tone, I seriously doubted he meant those words.

Her small, slender hand rested on her hip. "Thanks for watching while that punk had me pinned to the wall."

"If I had interfered, dear sister, you would have neutered me here in the club." He looked at me and added, "I'm damned if I do and damned if I don't. That's the way it's always been with her."

The woman didn't look shocked or hurt in any way—interesting. Perhaps this sibling banter was something she and Gabrihen had perfected over the years?

She glanced up at me. "Who's your friend?"

The roaming of her eyes from my feet to my head made me feel like a stud at an auction—lucky me.

"Zebastian," I said, meeting her cold gaze.

Her expression turned blank. "Zebastian?"

"The man you envisioned," said Gabrihen.

"That's not him." She said it with such conviction it made me laugh.

"What do you mean, Kaili? Of course it's him."

The other woman who resembled Kaili stood and offered her hand to me. "Hi, Zebastian. I'm Shaiya, Kaili's twin."

This woman was sweet and kind, an exact opposite of her twin. I accepted her hand. "Delighted to meet you."

Kaili stood. "This is not the man in my vision!"

Gabrihen gestured toward the door. "Let's take this outside, shall we?"

I allowed the females to follow their brother before bringing up the rear. Kaili gave me a suspicious look as she passed by. For such a tiny sprite, she sure had gumption. I'd never seen a female handle a male with such vigor. The rational part of me felt the thrill of a challenge I should avoid. The healthy male in me didn't care. Frigid or no, this female was intriguing.

Once we were out of earshot and eyeshot of the crowd, Gabrihen spun around to address his unruly sister. "This is the man you envisioned, Kaili. Now stop fooling around. We need your help."

I couldn't blame her for doubting it; I did too. She did not have the voice of the Angel who had stopped my rage—of this, I was certain.

"Who are you, really?" she asked me, poking a finger at my chest.

I grabbed her hand. "My name is Zebastian Carue."

She twisted and jerked her hand from my grip. "The man in my vision was different, more—furry."

"Change to your wolf," said Shaiya. "That will convince her."

"This is a waste of time," I told Gabrihen. "I'm out of here."

"Wait," said Gabrihen. "Tell her what happened. Tell her what she said to bring you out of your rage."

She stood back, hands on her hips and one leg slightly bent, her foot tapping the ground. "Yes, Zebastian, tell me those three perfect words that I said."

Clever girl. How could I have ever thought she was an Angel? "Not three perfect words, only one: 'Stop.'"

She stumbled back a few paces, looking as if she had swallowed something bitter. Then, she pulled a shiny object out of her bag and aimed it at me.

A bright light shone in my eyes, making me squint. "Jesus, what are you doing?"

"I need to see your eyes. That will convince me."

I stared down at her, ignoring the sting of the light.

She dropped the thing and stepped back. "It's you."

She looked down at the ground as if looking for words to mutter. "I imagined you—different."

"Imagined me?"

"She dreamt of you," Gabrihen explained, slapping me on the back. "You should be honored; it's further than any other man has gotten with her."

Kaili picked up her flashlight, turning it off before storing it back in her bag. "Thanks, Gabrihen." This time, there was pain in her tone. Her shoulders dropped, making her look defeated and vulnerable.

Gabrihen shifted, aware he had hit a sore spot. "That aside, we are here for a reason. Do you think you can put your attitude on hold for moment to help Zebastian remember a few things?"

Yes, good idea. The sooner we found their brother, the sooner I would have my freedom from this nightmare.

Kaili took a deep breath as if trying to calm the storm that spun in her mind. "Yes, of course." She turned to face me, her deep green eyes looking up into mine. When she reached for my hands, hers were shaking.

"I can't do this here."

"What? Why?" asked Gabrihen.

"I need somewhere quiet."

We all looked around at the dark woods surrounding us. Only a slight murmur of the crowd broke the silence.

"What's more private than this, Kaili?"

"The cabin. Take us there."

Gabrihen huffed. "The cabin? It's more crowded than this place. Are you crazy?"

"How about our place?" Shaiya suggested.

Kaili blushed, adding to a charm she had tried to keep hidden. "No."

"Where then?" asked Gabrihen, his voice diced with

impatience. Silence ensued. "Fine, your place it is then."

Chapter 8

~ Kaili ~

BY THE TIME WE REACHED the small house Father had purchased for Shaiya and me, Zebastian's face and knuckles had turned white.

He exited the car before Shaiya could even set the parking brake.

Gabrihen followed him out, shut the door, and then sauntered toward him. "You look a little peaked, my friend."

"Your sister drives like a blind moose."

"Hey," said Shaiya. "Let's try using nice words, shall we?"

"I was," said Zebastian.

She locked the car doors, and then led the way to our cozy home with a stone facade and gabled entrance. Gabrihen seemed to take it all in as if there would be a test later.

"Nice place," he muttered.

"Glad you approve," I replied from behind.

Shaiya opened the door and flipped on the lights.

Hanging her bag and coat on the pegs by the door, she continued into the living room. The men followed.

I carried my things to my bedroom and left them there. Breathe, I told myself. Ignore the fact that his black shirt shows every muscle and his jeans fit to perfection. Don't even think about those steel-gray eyes that look like a stormy sky.

I walked into the bathroom and splashed cold water over my face. Thank God I didn't wear makeup. "You can do this," I said to myself. "Just keep it simple, detached."

"Kaili, you want wine?" Shaiya called from the kitchen.

"Yeah, okay."

Whiskey would be a better choice—an entire bottle of it.

I walked out into the living room to find a cozy fire burning and the two men sitting on the couch sipping glasses of amber liquid, Black Bush by the looks of it.

Gabrihen's brow scrunched together. "You okay?" he asked me.

"Yeah, why?"

"Your shirt's all wet."

I looked down, feeling the color of my face match the bright pink material, now darker all the way down the center of my chest. "Right."

Returning to the sanctuary that was my room, I changed into something frumpy, less revealing, and definitely less—attention grabbing.

Zebastian's smile as I returned was not reassuring. "Now what?"

"Nice choice."

I looked down, trying to see what amused him. The shirt was gray, plain, and loose-fitting. It's three-quarter sleeves were comfortable and practical.

Shaiya came in with two glasses of red wine. "Are you cold?"

"No, why?"

"No reason." She handed me a glass before taking a seat across from the men. I joined her on the other chair.

Silence was comfortable in my world. Tonight, it felt disturbing. I cleared my throat. "So, Zebastian—"

"Please, call me Ze."

I nodded slowly. "Um ... Ze, tell me what you remember."

He turned the glass in his hand as he recounted the past day's events. Most of the details came telepathically, which was typical in the company of Spirians. Words were just too empty when it came to talking about anything complicated. His thoughts, however, were those of his wolf, and they went deeper than anything his human side remembered.

One of my gifts enabled me to understand animals, hence my desire to become a vet. Their form of communication encompassed not only sight, sound, and smell, but emotions and instincts that humans could not possibly comprehend. Animals saw things differently, as if observing life from another dimension.

"Your wolf scented someone; a man of power," I said.

Ze's eyes glowed against the firelight, polished steel with shards of sapphire. "How do you know this?"

"It's one of her gifts," said Gabrihen. "She talks to animals."

Ze laughed. "Like Doctor Dolittle?"

I narrowed my eyes at him. "Very funny."

He then sent me thoughts from his wolf that no mongrel, no matter how indecent, should be thinking. I stood and turned toward the kitchen, desperate to hide the blush that heated my face. I could feel him smiling.

Needing a reason for the sudden departure, I refilled my glass of wine. I returned to find each of them staring at me. Looking Zebastian straight in his steely eyes, I said, "Your thoughts are inappropriate and not appreciated in the least."

Shaiya looked confused. "Thoughts? What thoughts?"

"What are you talking about, Kaili?" asked Gabrihen.

I gestured to Ze. "He knows."

"Hey, I had to be sure."

"Did I miss something good?" asked Shaiya, always on the lookout for juicy tidbits to add to her perverted thoughts.

"Absolutely nothing," I assured her.

Gabrihen rolled his eyes and took a long pull from his whiskey. "Should we get on with it?"

"Are you sure you want to do this?" I asked Zebastian.

"You're just helping me remember, right?"

"To do that, I need to connect with you and reach into something you may consider sacred."

He stiffened. "Like what?"

"I will know your secrets, your fears, and you will know mine. Nothing will be hidden."

"I think the question is better aimed at you, then, angel. Do you really want to know my nightmares?"

"No, I don't, but if it helps us find Zhentu, it will be worth it."

"Let's do this, then."

I set my wine down and knelt before him. "I need to take your hands."

He offered them to me. Mine looked tiny in comparison, fragile almost. I pressed my palms against his, immediately feeling his warmth, his strength. His fingers curled around mine.

"Okay," I said, my voice quaking. "Now look in my eyes."

The connection was immediate, striking me in the center of my being like a bolt of lightning. Though his body convulsed, he kept his eyes on mine, wrapping my soul with a shield that felt protective and warm.

Images came, men with lab coats, taser rods. I jolted as I felt their sting over and over. Emptiness consumed me as the scent of fear, sickness, and death assaulted my nostrils. Needles jabbed at my skin, my mind whirled with emotion, confusion, and things that didn't make sense.

Zhentu, I called in my mind, *where are you?* Flashes of his eyes, his distinctive silver eyes, shone through the dark, framed by the mask of a gray wolf. I looked around through Ze's vision. The walls were dark and gray, built from stone. The scent of lead was heavy and prominent, making my stomach roil.

Voices echoed in the distance, followed by a familiar scent: sage and redwood. I had smelled that scent before, once when I was younger. Was it Ze's memory, or my own?

"This one is resistant," said a man. His white coat was stained with blood, darkening the letters SOAR. "He no longer reacts to the drug."

"Get rid of him, then."

The figures and faces blurred by the drugs and dim light stopped by Zhentu's cage. "What about this one?"

"His blood carries irregularities that could be helpful."

"And his reaction?"

"Controlled. He is strong."

The man asking questions made notes before moving to Zebastian's cage. "And this one?"

"His rage is deadly, and he remembers nothing."

"Excellent. Move him to Northup. They have a new serum to test."

Having felt enough, I released Ze's hand and broke the connection. My face was drenched in sweat and my heart felt ready to burst from my chest.

Shaiya rushed to my side. "Kaili!"

Ze looked as if he were in a trance, staring at nothing.

"I'm fine," I said, waving my hand before Ze—no response. "Ze, we're done." I slapped his face once, and then again with more force. "Zebastian!" I shook him. Still, he continued to stare.

"What's wrong with him?" asked Gabrihen.

"I don't know. I've never seen this before."

Shaiya placed my hands back into his. "Bring him back, Kaili. He's stuck in his memories."

Again, I made the connection. Shaiya was right. Ze was stuck. He had placed himself in some sort of trance to deal with the memories that he tried to forget.

Zebastian, I called to him, *listen to me. You're okay. Come back to me now.* No response.

His heart slowed and weakened, his breathing ceased. He was dying. *Stop!* I shouted mentally. After a few agonizing seconds, his breathing increased, his heart rate returned to a slow and steady rhythm.

Ze blinked, his hands gripping mine as if he would fall away should they let go.

"That's it," I whispered. "We're done. It's over."

He bolted from the chair and rushed to the bathroom.

"Is he all right?" asked Shaiya, wincing as Ze purged his stomach.

"He's been through hell," I said. "He's taught himself to black it out."

"Did you find Zhentu?" asked Gabrihen.

"Yes, I saw him, but Ze had no sense of the location."

Ze returned, taking a long sip of his drink. "Did you find what you were looking for, Angel?" His voice was gruff and deep.

"Nothing I could make sense of."

He sat and stared up at the ceiling. "God, please don't tell me that was all for nothing."

Now it was my turn to get sick. I ran to my bathroom and closed the door. The images and feelings we shared came flooding back in full, vivid detail. The pain—such pain. He had endured silence for too many years, and dim light. My joints ached now and my muscles felt fatigued as if they had been in spasm for several hours.

When my stomach was empty and my head stopped spinning with things it wanted to forget, I cleaned myself up and wandered back to the living room.

Zebastian sat back in the recliner, with his hand on a half-empty glass of whiskey. Next to it was the bottle of Black Bush, now three quarters spent.

Gabrihen and Shaiya talked quietly by the fire that had been stoked and fed. It now blazed bright in the darkness, warming the space with an orange glow. Shaiya must have healed Gabrihen's lip because it was no longer red and swollen. Her healing abilities were no match for our mother's, but they grew stronger every year.

Shaiya's eyes sparkled. "Hey, you doing all right?" She handed me a glass of wine.

I raised my hand and shook my head. "No wine, not now."

I felt Ze look at me through thin slits. His energy drew me to him, connecting me in ways that felt kind of creepy. I glanced back at him.

He smiled. "Welcome to my nightmare," he grumbled.

"That's putting it mildly."

He handed me his glass of whiskey, offering to share. I took it, swigged some down, then handed it back, wincing as the fire made its way down my throat.

"Ugh! You're drinking this stuff neat? No water?"

He smiled and nodded. "The way I like it."

"That's just wrong."

Gabrihen grabbed the bottle and poured himself another portion. "Well, I hate to break up this little ditty, but I'm dying to know what you found out."

I frowned, thinking back on the horrors I had witnessed through Ze's wolf vision and senses. It was all so fresh and disturbing. "I found out what hell is like."

Ze huffed, and then took another swig of his drink.

Since he wasn't about to contribute, I continued. "I saw Zhentu. He was alive, but not himself."

"Where?" asked Gabrihen.

"The place was dark, made of stone, but nothing indicated a location."

Ze placed his glass on the table beside him. It was empty now. "They took me to Northup afterward. That means that Zhentu was in Pathagon."

"Where's that?" asked Gabrihen.

"West of Northup. Each time they moved me, we headed East. Their technology improved in the Eastern facilities. The security was more dense, and the drugs more powerful. Few shifters ended up at Northup. When I escaped, there were only seven of us. They all died."

Gabrihen reached over, pouring the last of the Black Bush into Ze's glass. "So now we need to find out where Pathagon is."

Chapter 9

~ Steed ~

THE WOMAN WAS TOUGH, MUCH tougher than anyone warned me about. When I accepted this assignment, I thought it would be easy money. Little did I know that it could end my career—possibly my life.

The short redheaded female muttered something into the phone before hanging it up. Her pale green eyes looked over at me. "Mr. Graves will see you now."

Bennet Graves, the most powerful Shadow on the East side of North America—I could feel the pulse of his energy before even stepping into the room.

He was a businessman, and his surroundings revealed his success. The Graves building was one of the tallest in New York. His business occupied the entire top floor. His office, alone, was as spacious as my Long Island house, and that was no shack.

The curved wall, constructed of picturesque glass, offered a magnificent view of the Hudson River. His thick curved desk, constructed of solid rosewood, faced the window, placing his back to the door.

"Come in, Steed," he called over his shoulder. "Sit." He gestured to a simple chair across from his desk.

An impressive liquor cabinet stood to the right, complete with shiny crystal glasses and a small refrigerator. To the left was a bookshelf that stretched from floor to ceiling.

I strode across the polished wood floors that looked exotic—zebra wood, perhaps? I sat across from him.

He was a distinguished-looking man with silver-streaked hair and cobalt eyes, reminding me of Richard Gere in *Pretty Woman*. Rumor had it, Bennet Graves was an elementist, but few experienced the extent of his gifts. Everyone, however, knew of his power.

"What news do you bring me?" he asked, hands folded before him, patient, waiting.

"I didn't get a chance to talk to the female."

His eyes reflected no emotion. "Is there a problem?"

"She's—aloof."

"Aloof?"

"The other twin seems far more accessible and willing. I could—"

"I want Kaili." He steepled his hands before him. "Although, perhaps abducting one will bring the other by default, yes?"

"Um, there might be an additional problem."

Silver brows arched with curiosity, giving them a look of curled metal. "Problem?"

"Their brother was there, which means Khalen is close."

Bennet laughed, flipping a pencil between one finger and another. "No doubt investigating the abduction of young shifters."

"There was another man there."

"Who?"

"I don't know."

The pencil broke, shattering between his fingers like fragile glass. "Then find out!"

"Yes, sir." I stood and quickly made my way out of his office. I wasn't quick enough.

"Steed," he purred, backing that velvet tone with a stinging projection of energy.

My legs felt ready to collapse. I held firm, however, not wanting to seem weak before a man who could crush me with a thought. "Yes, sir?"

"Khalen is not to interfere; are we clear?"

"I cannot kill him, sir."

"No," he laughed, "of course you can't. I want him alive, dear boy. I want him to be helpless as I ravish his family and take over his region."

A hollowness filled my belly at the sound of those words. I knew Bennet was planning something with those shifters he had been engineering, but taking out Khalen and his brood was suicide. "Yes, sir."

His bind released me and I exited the room. Was it too late to back out now? If I did, Bennet's men would find me. I didn't sign up to battle with Khalen. He was a powerful leader backed by an even more powerful family. My bones would be scattered between here and Scotland if I were linked to his downfall.

When I accepted this assignment, I agreed to capture Kaili so that Bennet could study her gift with animals. Now it sounded sinister. Bennet wanted more than Kaili. He wanted Khalen and his entire region. He wanted Khalen to suffer, but why? What was Bennet doing with those shifters, anyway?

As I exited the building, seven Shadows approached

me. I stopped, considered a quick illusion, and then scrapped the idea. Bennet knew my abilities. His thugs would override them without effort. As I thought that, I felt an energetic bind surround me, paralyzing my gifts.

"Can I help you, gentlemen?"

One of them slipped me a picture. When I saw my mate and two young daughters with tear-streaked faces and bound wrists, my heart pounded double-time. "What is this?"

"Mr. Graves wanted you to know the importance of this mission."

"I didn't sign up for this. I was to bring back the woman; that's all."

"Would you like us to inform him that you've changed your mind, then?"

They had my mate, my girls. "I need to speak with Mr. Graves."

The fat one with a black beard pulled his phone out of his pocket and pressed a button. Having heard Bennet answer, he said, "Yeah, he wants to talk to you."

He handed me the phone. "Mr. Graves?"

"Yes, Steed, what is it?"

"Why are you doing this? My mission was to find the woman and bring her to you."

"You are correct, and did you succeed?"

"Not yet."

"Are there further complications due to your inadequacies?"

"No. These complications happened on their own."

"Yes, well, if you feel you're not up for the task, Steed, I will take the money back that I have given you and we will part ways."

"And my family?"

"Think of them as interest for the money you owe me."

"I see."

"Yes, I hope you do. Shall I begin extracting the money from your account, then?"

"No, that won't be necessary."

"Very good then. I consider the matter closed." The click on the other end confirmed that the call had terminated. I handed the phone back to the fat man.

"Just to let you know," said the one with long hair and an overpriced suit, "your daughters are sweet." He licked his lips to emphasize his point.

"Touch them and I will have you bound and quartered."

They all laughed. The picture they had given to me burst into flames. I tossed it to the ground. The energetic bind around me vanished, along with the men.

I looked down at the ground where I had flung the burning picture. It, too, was gone. Sweat soaked my shirt and dripped off my forehead. I pulled out my phone and dialed home. No answer. I dialed Tracy's cell phone; again, no answer.

"Leave a message at the beep," her sanguine voice instructed.

"Tracy, it's me. Call me as soon as you get this." I ended the call.

I was a dead man, no matter how this played out. My clan fell under Bennet's rule. Even if I left, his blokes would hunt me down and kill me. My family would suffer, my father shamed and persecuted.

Curse the skills that earned me this job. I was a strategist with talent for charming and manipulating. Now it was time to play it out in full force. Kaili Dunning would cooperate whether she was willing or not.

Chapter 10

~Kaili~

I FELT STEED'S EYES ON me all through biology class. Thank God this was our last week before finals. His illusion portrayed a young man, but I sensed more years than he pretended to be. The man gave me the creeps. I was glad to leave when the class was over.

"Kaili, wait up."

I turned to see Steed running toward me, adjusting his oversized glasses back onto his nose.

"I'm late, Steed."

"To where? You don't have another class after this one." Seeing few people were in the hall, he used his illusion to change back into the dashing young man who turned many a female's head.

"I work at the local vet clinic part-time."

He frowned at my lie. "Which local clinic?"

"The one outside of campus."

"There is no vet clinic outside of campus, Kaili. Are you trying to avoid me?"

His strong hand clamped around my arm, swinging

me around to face him.

"That hurts, Steed. Let me go."

"No, I don't think so, Kaili." He said my name as if it were honey on his tongue. I knew the tricks of illusionists and avoided looking into his eyes, rejecting the thoughts he pushed at me.

He laughed. "I know what you like, sweet girl. You want a man to take charge and step up to the plate with vigor."

He leaned in to kiss me. My knee aimed for his crotch, but this time he had anticipated it and maneuvered himself between my legs. His mouth crushed over mine, tasting like bitter coffee.

Trapped between his body and the wall, I didn't have much room to maneuver. Hitting him at this distance would be ineffective. The first time I waylaid him, I had the element of surprise. This time, he was ready for me.

"You're a spirited one," he growled in my ear. "I like that." The aroused scent he emitted confirmed that admission. It made my stomach roil.

Again, he claimed my mouth, his tongue forcing my lips to part. I parted them, and then bit down so hard on his tongue, my teeth drew blood.

He pulled back, screaming with rage. Before he could shove me back against the wall, I stepped aside and used his forward momentum to slam his head into the hard stone surface. It was enough to stun him. Thank God no one witnessed it. I assumed he had placed an illusion in the hall that caused people to avoid the passage.

"Wait!" he yelled as I bolted. A groan and a slur of curses followed.

I ran now, straight for our house. He didn't know where we lived and it was only a mile North of campus. I felt safe there. Father's wards had a lot to do with that I was sure.

I CLOSED THE DOOR BEHIND me and secured the deadbolt. Sweat clung to my clothes and dampened my face and neck. I needed a shower.

Looking into the mirror, I spotted a dribble of blood trailing its way from my lower lip. Great, Steed's teeth had bitten through my flesh. Now it looked red and swollen like I had taken a punch.

Spirian males turned aggressive when sexually frustrated, which was why it was so important for them to copulate frequently. Females were different. We had to be attracted to a male. That never seemed to be an issue with Shaiya, but for me, it formed a barrier. I never felt the attraction, which made my family suspect my orientation.

I took my shower and dressed in a comfortable pair of pink sweats. Now was a good time for a cup of joe and studying—anything to take my mind off Steed and his violent advances. My body shivered with the memory of his touch.

Sitting on the couch with a thick copy of *Biology, Second Edition* opened on my lap, I heard Shaiya's keys rattle in the door. My lesson on the endocrine system would have to wait.

She came in, dumped her stuff on the table, and then disappeared into her room.

I stood to follow her. "Shaiya. Is everything all right?"

When she turned to face me, my breath caught in my throat. Her face was beaten and bruised, her arms purple and battered.

"Good God, what happened?"

She reached over and touched my lip. "I could ask the

same of you."

"That fabulous male you picked out for me tried to make his move."

She scoffed. "Yeah, that same bastard tried to hit on me after dance class. When I refused his advances, he got rough."

"Please tell me he looks worse."

She leaned into the mirror and examined the damage. "You're not the only one with mad fighting skills, dear sister. The man won't be having sex for quite some time, I assure you. That pretty face of his will need some stitches as well."

"Stitches?"

"I hit him in the face with a barbell."

"Ooh, ouch. Well, get cleaned up. I'll pour you a glass of wine."

"That sounds good."

I walked out to the kitchen and then froze when a knock pounded against the front door. Shaiya had just gotten into the shower. Padding toward the door, I noticed she had left it unlocked. Heartbeats pounded in my ears as if I sat in a drum at the hands of a mad percussionist. Had Steed followed her here?

I placed my hand on the deadbolt and slammed it closed before peering through the peephole. No one was there. I heard nothing but my own pounding heartbeat. Paranoia had a way of messing with the head. Still, my instincts remained sharp.

My phone in the living room vibrated and chimed the dulcet tones of Beethoven's "Fur Elise." I ran over to check the display. No caller ID. The tune continued to play. I let it go to voicemail.

It rang again. I didn't answer it. The lock on the

front door began to turn. My heart slammed in my chest, fueling my brain to think. I picked up the poker from the fireplace and poised it over my shoulder.

The front door opened. A leather-clad boot stepped in. I hid behind the wall that separated the kitchen from the living room.

"Kaili? Shaiya?"

The voice was Ze's. I stepped around the corner, the fire poke still resting upon my shoulder. "Ze? God, what are you doing here?"

He stepped in and locked the door behind him. "A man followed Shaiya home; I saw him snooping around. I called, heard your phone ringing, but you didn't answer."

"Did you knock on my door?"

"No, why?"

The pressure of my throbbing blood made my head want to explode. I needed to sit down. "Someone did, just before you called me." I set the poker down and sat on the couch.

I looked down at my phone. "Your caller ID is blocked."

He raised the iPhone in his hand. "It's new. I haven't set it up yet. Your father insisted that I take it. He then gave me his car and told me—no, ordered me to keep an eye on you." His eyes focused in on my lower lip. "What happened?"

"I'm fine."

"You're not fine." He brushed his thumb over my lip, leaving a trail of tingles in its wake, and an unfamiliar need in my belly. "Who did this to you?"

I stepped back from his touch. "Jeez, you're starting to sound like my brother. I told you; don't worry about it."

The shower turned off. "Hang on. I need to tell Shaiya you're here or she'll come out without a stitch of clothing."

"I'm okay with that."

Groaning over that comment, I poured a glass of wine and carried it into Shaiya's room. When I came out again, Ze had helped himself to a cup of coffee and was stoking the fire.

I looked out the window, but the overgrowth of bushes and trees impaired my view.

"He left when he saw my Escalade."

"Father gave you the Escalade?" I thought for a moment, remembering that Ze had been in a cell for the past twelve years. "Do you even know how to drive?"

"Not really. It's more difficult than it looks."

He was serious. Was Father not thinking right? "Where's Gabrihen?"

"With Teak. They're checking out a few locations where Teak saw the transport trucks."

"Why aren't you with them?"

"Khalen wanted me here. He said he had a feeling and it turned out he was right."

Shaiya came out with her glass of wine in hand. She had put on a simple dress. Her face looked better, but still sported some cuts and bruises, which didn't escape Ze's notice.

He looked at me and then back to Shaiya. "Who did this?"

Her face paled as she realized she had forgotten to heal herself before stepping out of her room. "Oh, um."

"Steed followed you home," I told her.

Her face paled another shade, making her look like an ad for Mr. Clean.

Ze placed his coffee cup down on the small table at

the end of the couch. "Did he do this?"

She sank down on the chair, nearly spilling her wine. "Yes, it was Steed, the man you saw with Kaili at The White Stag. He tried to hit on me, and when I refused him, he got—persistent."

Ze growled, a deep throated growl that rumbled the walls. His steel-gray eyes focused on me. "You too?"

"Yes, he was quite persistent."

Shaiya set her wine down and buried her face in her hands. "God, I'm so stupid."

"Hey," I said, "you didn't know. He's an illusionist, Shaiya; he could make you see anything he wanted."

"I just wanted you to have a man, ya know?"

Great, that comment was something she could have kept to herself. I walked over and wrapped my arm around her trembling shoulders. "It's all right. We're safe now."

Ze pulled out his phone, frowning as he fumbled through the screens. He stepped outside to talk, obviously not wanting us to hear the conversation.

I placed my sister's hands over her beautiful face, now swollen and red from crying. "Heal yourself, Shaiya. You'll feel better." She did, and then she proceeded to heal my lip.

When Ze returned, he was frowning. "I'm to stay with you."

"That's ridiculous," I said. "Father has wards all around this place. If Steed has ill intents, he will not be able to enter. Shaiya and I are safe here."

"Look, this isn't what I want, either, but to get what I want, Khalen must get what he wants first; got it?"

"No. What are you talking about?"

"Let's just say I need to earn the right to continue living."

"Earn the right? Ze, what are you talking about?"

"I did something horrid that labeled me a monster. You saw it; you were there."

"Your rage?" I ventured.

He nodded.

"How does that make you a monster?"

He looked at me, the sapphire specks in his eyes dim with grief. "I killed my brother."

Shaiya took a sip of her wine and groaned. She hated drama, always did. "If Father believed you were dangerous, do you really think he would ask you to guard his daughters?"

"Did you not hear what I said?"

I motioned him to sit on the couch. "If you blackout in your rage, how do you know you killed your brother?"

"His blood was in my mouth. His throat was torn open by my teeth."

"The black wolf?"

"Yes, that was my brother. You saw what I did to him."

"You didn't kill him, Ze. The Guard did. I yelled, 'Stop!' as he was slicing his blade through the black wolf's neck. That was just before he turned, pulling your brother on top of him. You were going for the guard's throat, not your brother's. The guard used your brother as a shield against you. He didn't hear me, but you did." I frowned, thinking of something else.

"What?" asked Shaiya.

I looked over at Ze, who looked as if he had choked on a bug. Tears glistened in his eyes.

"Ze, are you all right?" I moved closer to him, shaking him gently. "You didn't kill him, Ze."

He reached over and pulled me into a rib-crushing hug. It felt wrong, yet right at the same time. He sobbed against my shoulder. I looked over at Shaiya, her eyes sparkling with hope.

I gave her the look that stated, "Don't think too much of this, dear sister."

After what seemed like several minutes, Ze pulled back from me, wiped his eyes and sat back against the couch. "I'm sorry. I don't fall apart like that ... ever."

"It's all right. Do you feel better now?"

"In some ways yes, in another, no."

"Explain."

"The guard, the one who killed my brother ..."

"Yeah?"

He thought for a moment, his brows knit in concentration. "He died. I never touched him. Others died as well."

"You had other shifters with you, yes?"

"They were dead."

"Oh."

Shaiya took another sip of her wine. "That's a little creepy."

My phone began to ring. The caller ID said Khalen. "Hi, Father."

"Is Zebastian with you?"

"Yes. Is everything all right?"

"I had ... visions. I need you and Shaiya to do as he says, understand?"

"Uh, sure. What kind of visions?" I winced after I said it, knowing better than to ask. He rarely discussed what he sensed with anyone except Mum.

"My insights are not concrete, Kaili; you know that. I just don't want to take any unnecessary chances."

"We need to attend our classes."

Silence ... never a good sign. "Understood. Just stay

safe and be aware."

"Um, okay. You too."

"Love you, Baby."

"Love you too, Father."

The call ended. I looked down at the phone as if it would offer some explanation. It didn't.

"What's up?" asked Shaiya.

"Father sounds worried."

Her eyes did the roundabout. "And that seems odd to you?"

She had a point. Father was always a bit on the over-protective side, but somehow, this felt different. "He wants us to be aware."

"Aren't we always?"

I looked over at Ze, who drank his coffee in silence. "I'm sorry I got you involved in this."

"You didn't. I became involved the day I escaped that damned mansion."

Shaiya stood. "Well, I have a final to study for, so I'm going to retire to my room."

She never studied for finals, and it was only six o'clock. "Aren't you gonna watch *Bones?*" It was her favorite TV show. She never missed it.

"I'll watch it in my room. Good night." She smiled over at Zebastian. "Good night, Ze."

He smiled back as if they were playing out a perfect scheme.

"Aren't you going to eat?" I said, watching her leave.

"Nah, I had something earlier. You two eat without me."

I looked over at Ze. "Have you eaten?"

"I caught something earlier today. I'm good."

"Caught something?"

He smiled and the blue flecks in his eyes lit up like tiny gems. "My wolf is a very good hunter."

I shuddered. "Right."

So, what was it about this guy that had my inner female drooling for attention?

From the kitchen, I asked, "So, where are you staying tonight?"

"Here," he replied, with a casualness that should not have come so naturally.

"Here?" I choked. We had only two rooms.

"Yes, I'm to stay with you, remember?"

I smiled. "Can you hand me my phone, please?"

Chapter 11

~Zebastian~

THE CONVERSATION BETWEEN KAILI AND her father sounded heated. Khalen, however, got the last word and Kaili ended the call with a heavy sigh.

"Is everything all right?" I asked.

"What kind of deal did you make with him, anyway?"

"Who, your father?"

"Yes, of course my father, who else?"

I drained my glass and settled back against the couch, looking into her heated emerald eyes. "I agreed to help him find Zhentu, and he agreed to let me live."

"Why would he kill you?"

I did not want to have this conversation with her, not tonight. For now, I wanted to get to know her, feeling intrigued by the softness she masked behind such a harsh attitude. It was time to change the subject.

"Do you always call Khalen, 'Father'?"

She poured me another serving of Black Bush before settling onto the couch beside me with a glass of Pinot Noir. "Yeah, what else should I call him?"

"Da, Dad, Pop, you know, something less formal."

She laughed, a sound I could immerse myself in forever. This female awakened things in me that left me stumped; visceral things that made my sex ache. Sitting on the couch in blue jeans was suddenly uncomfortable.

"Father is very old school, you might say. He doesn't like nicknames, abbreviations, or informal addressing of any kind."

"He sounds like my father. It almost drove him crazy when Teak started calling me 'Ze.'"

"Yeah, I bet. Well, don't expect my father to call you that name. You will always be Zebastian to him."

"What about your brother?"

"He's like father. At times, I think they act more like twins than Shaiya and I."

We continued conversing over mundane things, her school, and her desire to be a veterinarian for exotic animals. We then talked about our childhoods and how they were very similar, being the children of clan leaders.

"My father sees something special in you."

That got my attention. "Why do you say that?"

"He trusts you, and talks about you as if he knows you. That's very unusual for him. He's what most people consider ultra conservative, especially when it comes to strangers."

"Well, maybe he's wrong about me."

Her forehead creased in the middle, accentuating the bow-like arch of her thin blonde brows. "He's never wrong; not about stuff like that."

I took a lingering sip of my whiskey, enjoying the burn as it slid down my throat, warming my stomach. "I'm unpredictable."

She scoffed, tucking her feet beneath her. "You seem

fairly predictable to me, Zebastian."

"You haven't seen me angry."

"I believe I have." She finished the last of her wine and yawned.

I glanced up at the digital clock on the wall. It was almost midnight. "Wow, it's much later than I thought."

She nodded, not appearing surprised by the late hour. "I have an early class tomorrow. I'd better get some rest." She stood, then hesitated, before leaving. "I can give you one of my blankets, and my pillow. Is the couch going to be all right for you?"

I almost laughed. I had spent years sleeping on cold stone floors. This was luxury in comparison. "I'll be fine, Kaili. I don't need a blanket or a pillow."

Her look of confusion was adorable. "Um, okay. Good night, then."

"Good night."

She padded her way to her bedroom and closed the door. The scent of her lingered, making my body hunger for something denied for too long. Groaning, I stood to restock the fire. Absorbing its warmth, I curled up in front of it and closed my eyes.

I AWOKE TO A SCREAM. Sitting up, I listened. Everything was quiet, calm. The pounding of my heart lessened as I slowly realized that I must have been dreaming.

Stiff from having slept on the floor, I rose, stretching my aching back, hips, and legs until they were able to move without pain. The house was still, almost too still for my comfort. I walked around, glancing out through the windows, alert to any movement that caught my eye.

A knowing nagged at my instincts. Something was wrong. Looking at Kaili's closed door, I stood before it and listened. A slight whimper broke the silence. A scent, unfamiliar but laced with adrenaline, seeped through the cracks.

I turned the handle and pressed the door open. Kaili sat on her bed, knees drawn up toward her chest. Her window was open, the sheer white drapes fluttering in the cold and subtle breeze.

I rushed over and looked out the window. A man lay on the grass, moaning and rocking from side to side. I shifted into my wolf and launched myself out the window. By the time I landed on the soft grass, the man had disappeared. His scent still lingered, but his body was gone. A wizard, perhaps?

After a quick assessment, I ensured the man was gone and that it wasn't just an illusion. His scent had faded and there was no trace of his energy lingering. With an effortless leap, I bounded up through the window and shifted back to my human form.

Kaili sat there, eyes wide in amazement but clouded in fear. Ignoring the fact that I was naked, I closed the window and crawled onto the bed, pulling her quivering body into my arms.

"What happened?" I whispered, holding her close.

"A man. I've never seen him before. He came through my window. My father's wards must have shocked him because he shrieked in pain and grabbed my hair. Before he could drag me out the window, I poked my fingers into his eyes. He let me go."

"Khalen's wards should have killed him."

She nodded before breaking down with another wrack of sobs. "He was so strong. His eyes were evil, Zebastian, almost beastly."

I held her, gently kissing the top of her head. "You're

all right now, Kaili. I'm here."

Strands of her golden hair tangled in my hands, loose from having been pulled from her scalp. She had enough of the stuff, so I didn't think the loss would be too noticeable.

"This place isn't safe for you anymore."

"My father's wards are strong, Zebastian; what could have enabled that man to come in?"

In my gut, I knew what could enable a man to survive that kind of shock. I, myself, had been exposed to it over and over again by those SOAR bastards. The scent of that man was familiar. Had I scented it before?

"I should take you and Shaiya to the cabin."

"No," she sniffled. "Please don't."

"Why? Your father is there. He can protect you."

"So can you," she whispered. "So can you."

I held her tight, praying she was right. I had failed so many times in the past to protect those in my charge. What if I failed this time and something happened to Kaili or her sister?

"Stay with me, please?"

I lay down beside her, holding her in my arms, waiting for her soft breath to slow and deepen. Her heart calmed and the acrid scent of adrenaline eased away. Would she remember this come morning, or would she wake to remove my head from my body?

KAILI SHIFTED AGAINST ME. ONLY the thin sheet and blanket separated her backside from my aching need. I slowly pulled away from her. She stirred, pulling me back, her tiny grip like a vice around my arm. I needed to get out of this bed and dress before she woke.

She turned, facing me with dreamy eyes, still glistening

with sleep. A small smile stretched over her lips, giving her an angelic appearance.

"You're here," she whispered, gently grabbing my face in her hands and pulling me toward her. "Kiss me," she pleaded.

Not one to pass on an opportunity, I obliged her. I pressed my lips to hers, fighting the urge to take more. Her lips parted, inviting me in. I allowed it to feed my hunger and gorged myself in her sweetness, tasting her tongue and lips.

Her body arched toward me, her hands roaming over my skin like silk in a subtle breeze. Eyes closed, she moaned as if caught in a dream. Was she dreaming?

Feeling my control slip and weaken, I grabbed her wrists and held them over her head. "Kaili, look at me."

Her eyes fluttered open. When they were finally able to focus, they widened and her pulse slammed against her tender neck. I wanted to kiss it there at that spot, but her changing scent warned me to rethink the idea.

"Zebastian?" She tried to free her wrists, something I wasn't about to allow until her wits were solid.

"Calm down, and I'll let you go."

Again she struggled. Her legs flailed, forcing me to straddle them. "Kaili, calm down!"

"Get off of me!" She struggled, groaned, and cursed until her strength was spent.

"What do you remember?" I asked.

"Let me go!"

"Not until I know you are calm."

Again, she thrust and fought my hold, an impossible feat against the strength of a shifter. "Tell me what you remember."

Her brow sweaty now from her efforts and her chest

heaving, she growled like a threatened kitten. Her body finally relaxed, but I knew better than to let down my guard. My hold on her remained firm.

"You're hurting me, Zebastian."

I loosened my hold and felt her shift. Clever little minx. I kept my instincts sharp, open to any change in her energy. If she were going to make a move, I would be ready. "Fight me again, Kaili, and I will not release you until I'm good and ready. Understand?"

I could almost see the gears turning in her pretty little head.

"Why are you doing this?"

"Because, you woke up and asked me to kiss you. I did. Then, you became more—adventurous. I wanted to make sure you asked for my affections and not those of someone in your dreams."

Her face flushed with a new kind of heat that had nothing to do with exertion. She licked her lips.

"Why are you naked?"

"Because a man tried to take you last night and I went after him. When I shifted back, I didn't bother with my clothes because you were shaking."

She nodded, her eyes darting back and forth as if recounting the events in her mind. "Yes, I remember." Her eyes roamed over my body. "I need you to put some clothes on."

"I will, when I know you're aren't going to kill me as soon as I release you."

"I won't."

I eased off her, watching her body language for any signs of attack. She watched me don my clothes as she rubbed at her wrists.

"You're incredibly strong, Zebastian."

"Most shifters are."

"Zhentu was never that strong."

"Shifters don't gain their strength until they are mature males."

Silence filled the spacious room like a heavy fog. Part of me wanted to leave while another part wanted to know of whom she had been dreaming.

"Um, I need to get dressed now," she said, hinting that I take my leave.

"Who was in your dreams?"

She bit her lip and stared at the far corner of the room. "Why does it matter?"

"Was it me you asked to kiss you, or the man in your dreams?"

"I believe you know the answer, Zebastian."

I walked toward her, growing tired of her evasive game. Again, her pulse quickened, but it was not from fear. No, this woman was excited by me, by my strength— interesting.

I pulled her against me, capturing her delicate face in my hand. She didn't fight me. Drawing closer to her lips, I asked again in a low, throaty whisper, "Was it me, Kaili, or someone else?"

She swallowed hard against my hand, the pupils in her eyes softening with desire. "It was you."

With that, I pressed my lips tenderly over hers, spurred by the fact that her arms wrapped around me as if she were a woman drowning, desperate to be saved. Neither of us ended the kiss.

If I didn't end it soon, however, I would not be able to stop from taking her here and now. With hesitation, I pulled away, both of us breathing hard.

"I should get ready for school," she said.

"Yeah, good idea."

Chapter 12

~ K a i l i ~

ZEBASTIAN WAS GONE BY THE time I got out of the shower. The note he had left on the counter assured me he would return that evening.

Shaiya had been shocked at the news of my near abduction, but she was more interested in Zebastian's act of chivalry. I kept my recounting very generic and mild, though it was anything but that. The man was powerful, confident, and...

My phone rang with Ze's name showing on the caller ID. "Hello?"

"You're thinking of me," he said.

"And how, pray tell, do you know that?"

"I'm tapped into your thoughts, making sure you arrived at class without incident."

I wasn't sure whether I felt pleased or annoyed. Annoyed, I finally determined. "Well, I did, and now you can exit my thoughts with as much grace as you obviously entered them."

"Don't be angry, kitten; my job is to protect you,

remember?"

"First, this kitten has claws, and second, I don't appreciate how you convinced Father to place wards around us that would fry anything that comes near?"

"Well, you can retract those claws, angel, because I'm here to stay, and those wards will be with you until we find out what's going on."

"Just remember, Ze, you are not immune to my father's wards."

"They only react when you feel threatened and I am not a threat."

"Don't be so sure." I pressed the end button, leaving him with something to think about. How dare he enter my thoughts without my permission. How did he do that, anyway?

~ Z e b a s t i a n ~

THE FEMALE WAS A BOLT of lightning seeking an easy ground. I wasn't about to give it to her—something we would discuss later this evening, whether she wanted to or not.

This morning, she aroused me to the brink of control. Had she known how close I had come to taking her? Judging by her scent, she was more than ready for it, which only served to fuel my aching need further.

An eagle holding something in his massive claws screeched overhead, circling me before landing; it was Teak. After changing into his human form, he leaned down and retrieved a pair of jeans and a simple green tee-shirt from the bag he had in his claws. He came prepared.

"What?" he said, noticing my speculative glance.

"You carried your clothes with you?"

"I don't suppose you brought me any—that fit?"

I shrugged, thinking about the clothes I had stashed in the back of the car. "They might be a bit large."

He huffed. "Yeah, large in the girth and short in length. No thank you."

"So what did you find out?"

"The man, named Steed, met with someone associated with SOAR. I guess the meeting didn't go well because the moody illusionist left in a huff."

"How do you know he's associated with SOAR?"

Teak retrieved his bag and headed toward the Escalade. "Because he entered one of their unmarked transport trucks. The ones that look as if they came straight out of a military war zone; tan camo and decked to the gills with armor." He gestured to the silver Escalade. "Nice ride."

"It's Khalen's."

He tossed his bag into the back. "Well, I didn't think it belonged to you."

"Where are we going?" I asked, settling into the cab with him.

He fastened his seatbelt. "The Baymont Inn. It's where our boy, Steed, is staying."

After punching the address into the GPS, I pressed Route and allowed the synthesized voice of a female to guide us there. "Things have changed a lot over the past twelve years."

"It doesn't seem to have slowed you down any. I'm surprised Khalen let you drive this rig."

"I'm a fast learner."

"Always have been."

I let the compliment slide. Teak always did think too highly of me, even my father had said so on multiple occasions. "Any luck in finding Pathagon?"

"We'd have better luck finding a particular nerd at a Star Trek convention."

"Do they even have those anymore?"

His eyes grew wide as saucers. "Red light!"

I floored the gas pedal, weaving around a driver who had jumped the gun and wasn't paying attention.

"Jesus, Ze. Want me to drive? Please?"

"The bugger needs to pay attention and wait his turn."

"The light was red, Ze. That means you need to stop."

"It was yellow when I hit the intersection."

He took a deep breath and stared up at the cab ceiling as if asking the Father for patience—or perhaps something else.

I turned left onto Meridian, which made Teak grip the car door as if the thing were going to fly away.

"Khalen won't appreciate you leaving your finger dents on his leather door panels, my friend."

"Whatever possessed him to give you the keys?"

"Is there a problem?"

"That car almost hit you, Ze."

"That's his issue. I had plenty of room to turn."

He groaned and buried his face in his hand. "Just let me know when or if we get there."

Kellogg was just around the corner. I turned left, spotting Steed in the parking lot. I kept driving.

"Hey, you passed it," said Teak.

"Check out the guy getting into the black Firebird."

"That's him; that's Steed."

"Exactly, and he knows Khalen's rig."

Just then, Steed's head whipped around, following as we turned the corner.

"He spotted us," said Teak.

I spun the car around.

"He's heading north."

"Yeah, I've got him."

Accelerating after him, I wasn't too concerned about him knowing he had a tail. Our presence was no surprise. Apparently, he thought he could outrun us. We caught up to him at the light, and then poof, he was gone, just like that—no more Firebird.

"Where did he go?" asked Teak.

"He's an illusionist. He could be anywhere."

Teak shifted into his eagle and I opened the window. The last thing I wanted was his eagle claws digging into the leather interior. Out he flew, leaving his pile of clothes on the seat.

Illusions were ineffective on shifter animals. No one really understood why and it was rare, if not impossible, for shifters to have illusionistic gifts.

Telepathically, Teak sent me an image of Steed's car heading north. I kept the communication open between the eagle and me. Spirians could communicate telepathically for about a mile, but after that, the information became scattered and incomprehensible. For me, however, distance didn't seem to pose a problem. I supposed it had something to do with the serum the SOAR group had injected me with for so many years.

Mates could communicate over any distance because they shared a spiritual bond where two souls became one. It was a concept that I hadn't considered until today. Cocking an awkward smile, I relished how Kaili had me contemplating many things.

She would be a challenging mate—a fact that made me hungry to explore the notion further. In the recesses of my mind, I could almost hear Khalen arguing how

Kaili and I weren't old enough to form such a bond. Most Spirians didn't mate until they were thirty to fifty years old.

The next image I received from Teak showed the university campus. My heart pounded hard against my ribs. The girls would be out of class soon. Would Khalen's ward be strong enough to thwart an illusionist?

Through Teak's eyes, I witnessed Steed parking the car and talking to someone on the phone. He gestured with his hand for someone to go around. Who was he talking to? Teak must have thought the same thing, as he scanned the campus for movement. Two young students and a clumsy older male who couldn't hold the pile of papers and books he had balanced in his spindly arms was all he saw.

I parked the car and considered entering the campus, but as what? A wolf would cause alarm. My panther form was also not an option. Entering as a man would make me vulnerable to Steed's illusions.

I pinged Kaili telepathically, but she blocked me out. Using my cell phone, I dialed her number. It went straight to voicemail. I got out of the car and slammed the door so hard the windows rattled. "Bloody hell!" Kaili was in the science building while her sister was in the performing arts hall.

Teak lost sight of Steed when he entered a building. Teak was now heading toward me. I opened the door for him so he could shift without notice.

"What now?" he asked.

I gestured toward the building Steed had entered. "We try to find the girls before he does."

"He'll cast an illusion, and God knows who's working with him. I saw no one."

I thought for a moment. Going into the building would serve no purpose at all. "We'll wait for them out here. Shift back to your eagle; I'll shift to my wolf."

"What about the girls?"

"I'll break through to Kaili."

With a groan, he shifted and then took flight.

I tossed my clothes in before closing and locking the doors, stuffed the keys behind the front tire, and then shifted into my wolf. It wasn't the most inconspicuous animal, but it was one I connected with most and one that Kaili would recognize. I called out to her telepathically.

Ze?

In this form, I could only communicate in wolf speak, but it was a language she clearly understood. *Where are you?*

Still in class. Professor Blithe wants to speak with me.

I sent her images of Steed and other images that were blurred, indicating I didn't know who they were or how many.

Understood. Where are you?

I looked around for the parking lot sign.

You're in 11-G, she acknowledged. *I'll be right there.*

Call your sister to let her know. Do not trust anyone, understand? Keep your thoughts open to me, Kaili.

Okay.

Now it was a waiting game. Steed would make his move, Kaili would let me know, and then Teak and I would be ready.

Kaili sent me images of the building she traversed and the people she passed. I could feel the sharpness of her instincts and the flow of her blood as it pumped through her veins. The connection I had to her was unusual, seeing we were not related by blood or union. I assumed it was her gift that connected us, and I wondered whether she had that same connection to all animals.

Her pulse quickened and she felt alarmed. Someone was tailing her and closing the distance fast. I alerted Teak and started running toward Building 43. She would be exiting through the north door.

"Kaili," I heard a deep male voice speak through her ears.

Don't turn, I told her. *Keep moving. I'm almost there.*

She burst through the door, panting and flushed. When she spotted me, I felt a sense of relief. No one followed her out.

"I couldn't reach Shaiya."

Come on, I communicated, running alongside her toward Building 16. Before we could reach the staff parking lot, Kaili froze. Her mind sent images of an immovable crowd of people.

It's an illusion, Kaili; keep moving. Grab my scruff and close your eyes if you need to, but ignore what you see.

I felt her grip my fur, keeping pace with my lengthy stride.

"Cool dog," a student said as we ran past. Others just stared. Kaili was in a fog, her mind clouded by illusions. What kept her feet moving in the midst of them was nothing short of a miracle. Images of nightmarish proportion flashed through her mind, eliciting childlike whimpers from her as we continued to run. We crossed Highland Drive, cutting through the bus terminals.

Kaili sagged to the ground, gasping as if she had swallowed something too big for her throat.

It's an illusion, I reminded her. She didn't respond.

Above us, Teak screeched, sending me images of Shaiya being led to a car. She, too, was under an illusion.

Stop them, I instructed.

Chapter 13

~ S t e e d ~

I **LOOKED ON AS THE** wolf shifter hovered over his precious charge like a moth guarding the flame that would eventually kill it. He couldn't save both females, now could he? I took my cell phone out of my pocket and dialed the henchmen Bennet had awarded me. They doubled as my executioners as well, should things fall out of line.

"Yeah," the voice of Stewart answered. He was a brilliant bastard with looks that mimicked Tom Cruise in *Mission Impossible* after he had bulked up for the role. Unlike Cruise, however, Stuart did not do his own stunts. That was his sidekick, Joth's, job.

"Get a read on him while his eagle friend is hovering over the lure."

Shifters may not be susceptible to illusions, but they were not infallible. Joth was one of Bennet's special projects, so to speak; a guinea pig with incredible talents but absolutely no brains. He had the ability to morph one thing into another, making the observer believe they were seeing something else; an illusionist, but trickier. The eagle believed he saw the twin being escorted from the building, when in reality it was another poor girl altogether.

"The bloke is chipped," reported Stewart. "Number 6169."

Perfect, I thought. We were facing off with one of Bennet's super shifter escapees—a killer without a conscious. "Very good. Call Joth off and report back to the hotel. We need to move our stuff. Our location's been compromised."

"Understood," said Stewart.

My next call was to Bennet Graves. His secretary answered on the third ring then promptly placed me on hold. Bennet answered a minute later.

"Steed."

"Mr. Graves. The man you inquired about is chipped with number 6169." Silence followed, filled only by the subtle clicks of a computer keyboard.

"I want him alive, understand?"

Frowning, I shook my head. Was the man crazy? "Sir, that might not be possible."

"Drug him if you have to, Steed, but bring him in alive, along with the two girls."

The rules were changing faster than I could keep up. "Both of them?"

"Yes, I believe that is what I said. Are you having a problem with your hearing?"

I took a deep breath, cursing my stupidity for ever getting into this mess. "No, Sir. I heard you just fine." Click. The phone went dead.

Releasing my illusion on Khalen's daughter, I returned to my car. It would have been easier to let her choke to death, but that would not please Bennet by any measure, and right now, he had my nuts in a vice. To get my family back alive, I would have to comply with this insane scheme. If I managed to survive it, my family and I were taking the first plane back to Australia. To hell with Bennet and his clan.

I got into my car and slammed the door. Capturing the twins and the super shifter was going to take some planning. Going in willy-nilly was suicide, and getting myself killed was not going to help my family at all. I glanced up at the pesky eagle circling above me. He would have to be eliminated—soon.

~Zebastian~

SHE STARTED BREATHING AGAIN, HER brow soaked in sweat and her skin pale as cream. A crowd gathered around us, my growling wolf keeping them at bay.

"I've called 911," said one of the bystanders, a skinny guy with brown curly hair and a nauseating green and red striped shirt.

"Is that a wolf?" a short blonde gal asked, adjusting her glasses over her nose.

"Yeah," answered another gal, taller and skinnier, her long brown hair flowing over her shoulders. "I think he belongs to her."

I growled, indicating that I was not comfortable with the gathering crowd. *Kaili, can you stand?*

She looked around at the encroaching horde and nodded. *I think so. I feel dizzy, though.*

When she tried to stand, the skinny guy approached her and then backed away as I elicited a low growl.

"Whoa!"

"I'm fine," said Kaili.

"I called 911. They will be here soon," said skinny guy.

"No, I'm good, really."

On shaky legs, she supported herself against me and started walking. The crowd parted, giving us a wide berth.

Teak, where are you?

He sent me an image of the black Firebird heading south.

Leave him. Where's Shaiya?

He sent me brief flashes of what had happened with the girl he thought had been Shaiya. Growling, I told him to meet me back at the car.

Kaili was weak. After settling her in the cab, I donned my clothes. This, of course, elicited speculative stares from people passing by. At this moment, I didn't care.

Teak came, donned his clothes in the back of the car, and then emerged with a look of concern. "They'll be back, Ze."

"Yeah, I know. Stay here with Kaili. I'm going in to find Shaiya." I tossed him the keys. On the way to Building 16, I called Khalen.

"Zebastian."

"The Shadows came after the girls at school. It's not safe for them here, Khalen. I'm bringing them to the cabin."

"Understood."

I ended the call and hurried into the performing arts hall. Dancers milled about like bees on a warm spring morning. Music poured from one of the rooms so I headed there.

"Can I help you?" asked a pleasant female with flaming red hair and tight black leotards that left little to the imagination.

"I'm looking for Shaiya Dunning."

The woman looked me up and down, a slight smile indicating she approved of what she had inspected. After an awkward moment of silence, she gestured to the far end of the hall with her head. "Over there, dancing with Raymond."

"Thank you." I left her standing there, feeling as if she had cast some eerie web over my entire body from which I was just now breaking free. She certainly wasn't a Spirian, but dang if she couldn't emit some creepy vibes.

Shaiya danced like a dandelion seed in the wind, free, graceful, and light as a whisper. Her partner, on the other hand, looked like Arnold Schwarzenegger trying to handle a delicate butterfly as it was trying to fly away.

Frustrated and damp with perspiration, Shaiya glanced at me, concern washing over her delicate features. "Ze? Is everything all right?"

Raymond cursed. "We're kind of busy here, buddy; can you come back later? Like ... when rehearsal is over?"

Shaiya walked toward me. "What's going on?"

I looked over at her partner until he shifted uncomfortably and looked away. "Something's happened. I need you to come with me. Now."

"Okay." She glanced back at Raymond. "We're done for the day." Grabbing her bag, she followed me out of the room, ignoring the slew of curses flowing from Raymond's mouth.

"That guy is such a putz. If I never dance with him again, it will be too soon."

We walked down the hall and out the north entrance, Shaiya running to keep pace. "Ze, what's going on? Where's Kaili?"

"In the car. I'm taking you to the cabin tonight."

"Why? What happened?"

When she saw her sister lying down in the front seat, she ran toward her. "Kaili?"

Kaili raised her hand. "I'm fine, Shaiya, just a little nauseous."

Teak paced by the car, clearly agitated with having to be here instead of following Steed.

"Get in the car," I told him.

Shaiya climbed in behind Kaili, having enough sense to keep quiet. Both Teak and I were amped up. It wouldn't take much to push either of us over the edge.

Teak tossed me the keys and then sat in the backseat. "He's going to move, Ze, and his next attack will have reinforcements."

"I know that, Teak." My response came out a bit more harshly than intended.

"I should be following him."

I looked at him through the rearview mirror, slammed the car into gear, and then peeled out of the parking lot. "And do what? You saw how easy they duped you out there. They weren't after the females. They were after something else. The girls were decoys."

He sat back, pondering that thought for a moment. "You think they were after you?"

"No. But whatever it was, they left in a hurry and spared our lives. Something tells me we are missing the bigger picture here."

The rest of the short ride occurred in silence, something I really appreciated now. Kaili's color was deepening—a good sign. When we arrived at the house, Shaiya was the first to exit the car. I couldn't blame her, really. She had been wrenched from practice and hauled into the middle of a testosterone feud. Her sister looked worse for the wear and still Shaiya had no answers about what went down. I had to hand it to her. She knew when to stay on the down low instead of asking a slew of questions that had no answers. That said a lot for the female.

She opened Kaili's door and helped her inside. "I'll make you a cup of cocoa."

"I'm fine, Shaiya, really." Kaili walked beside her sister, both of them talking quietly to each other.

"No time for cocoa," I said, feeling like a calloused rogue. "Pack a few things. I'm taking you back to the cabin."

Kaili turned around. "What? Why?"

"Not now, Kaili. Please, just do as I ask."

We locked eyes for a few tense moments, before Shaiya convinced her to come inside.

Teak turned to face me. "Why am I here, Ze? I should be following Steed and his men."

"I have a bad feeling about this, my friend. For no other reason, I ask that you stay with us."

"What kind of bad feeling?"

One look from me had him backing up with his hands raised. "Right, okay. Bad feeling. Got it."

Chapter 14

~ K a i l i ~

MY FATHER PACED BEFORE THE hearth that separated the living quarters from the dining room. This place was called, "the cabin," but in reality, it was a small mansion. At 5,200 square feet, it housed eight people very comfortably. It resided near the Canadian border and harbored eight spacious rooms, five complete bathrooms, and a daylight basement game room where my uncles, Ian and Aidan, spent most of their time. They stood now, shooting pool with Gabrihen and his good friend, Connor, Elle's son.

Nothing good ever came from Gabrihen and Connor when they were together. They were the epitome of Dr. Jekyll and Mr. Hyde, only far more destructive. I remembered the last time they experimented in Father's surgery back home. They nearly obliterated the place. If Father hadn't been there to quench the explosion and flames, the entire camp would have been annihilated.

My mother sipped her wine, apparently unaffected by my father's insistent pacing. It was something she had grown accustomed to, I was sure. Maiyun, her guide dog, lay by her side. She was so old now that I often wondered how she had managed to survive so long. I was sure it had to do with the daily healing my mother offered her, as well as her infallible will to stay by Mum's side. The Malamute's eyes roamed left and right as she watched Father pace back and forth.

Okay, I couldn't take it anymore. "Father, please, sit down. We need to talk about this."

He stopped and pierced me with that golden gaze of his that would stop a raging rhino in its tracks. "The matter is closed, Kaili."

"I have finals this week. I cannot stay here. Shaiya has a performance. We—"

"You will stay here as Zebastian suggested."

"Ahg," I groaned, standing and pacing like my father before the hearth. "You treat him like family when he's nothing but a shifter with an attitude."

"Enough!" Father said. "Kaili, sit."

I turned to face him; his expression was one I didn't want to challenge now, so I did as he asked.

He paced a few more times, clenching his jaw and running his fingers over his tethered hair. "Kaili, I understand your frustration. Zebastian is new, and yes, he is unproven, reckless, and somewhat dangerous, but I trust him."

"Why? You don't even know him?"

Again, his eyes zeroed in, holding me in place. "And you do?"

"Yes, no—I mean..."

He burst into laughter.

"What?" I asked, flustered.

The laughing continued. I looked over at my mum,

who continued to sip her wine in silence, a smile stretched over her face. "Mum, please. Help me out here."

She looked over at me, her pewter eyes sparkling with pride that was clearly unmerited. "My dear, you sound like a woman in love. Your father is happy, that's all."

"In love? Good grief, I've known Ze for less than a week—hardly a foundation for love."

Both of them continued to look at me as if I were in denial. "This may seem a bit off topic, but I would like to bring up the subject of school, my finals, and the fact that we are two hours from campus."

"Zebastian wants you here," said Father, "and I agree with him."

"So that's it? End of story? My entire quarter pissed away without another thought?"

"Kaili!" Mum said, her voice laced in disgust. "Your life is worth far more than one quarter of studies."

"Easy for you to say. I pulled sixteen credits this quarter. I'm not going to walk away from it all because some Shadow has a bee up his bum."

"If I can arrange for you to take your finals, would you oblige us in this?" asked Father.

"Yes."

"Excellent. I will contact the Dean and arrange your exams."

"What about Shaiya and her performance?"

"She has not mentioned it."

"It's important to her, Father."

"I believe your sister can speak for herself."

I was going to lose this battle; I just knew it. Shaiya would not mention her performance; it was not her way. She was a pleaser, always doing what was expected of her, and not what she wanted in her heart. In that respect, we were like night and day. She always flowed with the tide, while I always swam against it. No wonder she had more men than I did.

Mum came over and sat on the couch beside me. "Kaili, I know this is hard on you, sweetie. Your father doesn't want to make your life miserable, believe me."

"I know, Mum, but I can't help wondering if Shaiya and I are ever going to have a normal life."

"Define 'normal,'" she laughed.

"You know, school, dating ... life. No other student in school has to worry about Shadows."

Father raised his brows and tended to the fire. "You and your sister chose to go to a traditional school, Kaili. Your friends are all human. At Edinburgh, we had plenty of squabbles with Shadows."

"Indeed," another voice said. I whipped my head around and saw Seth and his beautiful mate, Rae, standing under the archway that separated the living space from the dining hall. I ran toward him, nearly knocking him down with my embrace.

"Whoa," he said, bracing himself against the wall. "You've grown since I last saw ye." He pushed me back a little. "You've filled out some too. Let me have a look at ye." He spun me around like a doll on display. His Scottish accent was thicker now and he had done some filling out of his own.

Rae gently pushed her mate away. "Stop it, Seth. You're embarrassing her." She wrapped her arms around me and offered a sturdy hug.

"It's good to see you two," I said.

"We met your man, Zebastian. Fine choice, lass."

"My man?"

"Oh, aye. He made that point clear when I went up to

say boo to your sister."

Seth and Father exchanged glances. Mum just smiled. All of them acted as if they had some secret they all shared. With frustration, I groaned perhaps a bit too loud. "I hardly know him."

Just then, the devil in question entered the room, along with Gabrihen, Teak, and Connor. Ian and Aidan brought up the rear. In a room crowded with grown Spirian males, I felt like a mouse in a cage of hungry cobras.

"I'll unpack my things," I said, needing to escape the flow of testosterone. Rae and Mum must have felt the same way, seeing as they followed me out, Mum saying she had to see to dinner, and Rae offering to help.

How had Zebastian whittled his way into my father's heart so quickly? He was being treated like a bloody leader or something, yet he was around my age. What made him so special? I was sure that Gabrihen was thinking the same thing. And what was that bunk about him being my man? I huffed. Did he honestly think that one simple kiss was enough to bond me to him? If he did, he had another thing coming. Bonding or no, I had a choice of which man I belonged to, and many years to determine that fate.

I rounded the last corner of the long spiral staircase to the third floor. My room was down the hall and to the right, across from Gabrihen's—perfect. I would no doubt hear him and Connor play some sort of annoying role-playing game during the odd hours of the night. Honestly, the two of them were intolerable when they shared the same space. It was annoying.

I opened my door, the knotted pine floors creaking as I entered. I expected to see my bags on one of the two twin beds, but they were nowhere in sight.

"Hey," Shaiya said, peeking in through the door.

"Hi."

"What's with the frown?"

"Did you unpack my things?"

"No. Zebastian did."

Feeling my heart pound like a raged animal against its imprisoning bars, I walked to the closet and opened the sliding mirrored door. Six pairs of oversized jeans hung neatly on hangers, right next to mine. The look I offered Shaiya made her cringe.

"I guess no one told you."

"Apparently not. Care to explain?"

"Um, you and Ze are sharing a room."

My eyes widened like Wile E. Coyote's just before a train smashed into him. "No, we're not."

"There aren't enough rooms and my stuff takes up far too much space."

"Shaiya, I am not sharing a room with Ze."

She started backing out of the room. "It's just for a few days, Kaili, and then he'll be able to move into Seth's room. Ze said you wouldn't mind."

"He's sadly mistaken. I do mind and it's not going to happen."

Her eyes narrowed as if what I said didn't make sense. "What is your problem? It's not like you need to share the same bed or anything—not that that would be a bad thing," she added in a hushed voice. "Ze said he wanted to be close to you in case another Shadow tried to enter the house."

I followed her out of the room. "What idiot would be suicidal enough to enter this house, Shaiya? Between Father, Ian, Aidan, and Seth, the bugger wouldn't stand a chance."

"I think it's sweet that he wants to protect you." She

turned to face me. "He said that as your man, it was his duty," her voice dripping like a mouth full of sour candy.

Again with the "my man" thing. "He's not my man!"

She shrugged and curled her lips down, giving her a mock innocence that would have fooled anyone but me. "He thinks he is."

I pushed past her and ran down the polished pine stairs. Entering the room full of men discussing something that seemed to be intense, I pressed between Seth and Teak and walked straight up to Zebastian. "May I speak with you, please?"

"We're in the middle of a conversation, Kaili; can it wait?"

"No, it can't."

He actually looked down at me as if considering a no. I matched his cold stare with one of my own, backing it up with crossed arms and a foot that was ready to find its mark on his shin if necessary.

He then glanced over at Father. "Excuse me for a moment."

Father nodded.

Once we were out of earshot in the study, he turned me to face him, his grip firm on my arms. "Now," he said, his voice deep and pooling with anger, "what is so important that you had to interrupt our conversation?"

God, the smell of him had my knees weak and my heart pounding in my chest as if it wanted to get closer to him. I tried to step back but he wouldn't allow it. "Let me go, Zebastian."

He smiled. "You wanted my attention. Now, you have it."

I tried twisting out of his grip, stomping on his feet, kicking him, but the bugger was too strong and fast. I ended up on the floor with him on top.

"Entertaining as this all is, Kaili, I have more pressing matters to discuss. Are you done?" He wasn't even out of breath—infuriating.

Now his face was inches above me, those blasted steel-gray eyes locking onto mine like entrancing magnets.

"I am not your female," I growled, "and I am not sharing a room with you."

He laughed. "That's what this is all about?"

"It's hardly funny, Zebastian."

He stood with the grace of a warrior and hauled me to my feet as if I weighed no more than a blanket. Brushing the hair from my face, he looked at me like a man admiring a precious gem. He then proceeded to kiss me.

I tried pushing away, but the softness of his lips, the scent of his skin, and the warmth of his firm embrace had my body betray me with a will of its own. It melted into him, yielding to him with no consideration of my internal battles.

Slowly, he pulled away, a smile softening his features. "We'll continue this conversation tonight." With that, he released me and walked away.

Chapter 15

~Zebastian~

THE THOUGHT OF MY SPIRITED minx getting all flustered under my kiss was enough to make me forego the meeting and whisk her away to the room to discuss things further. Unfortunately, time did not allow for that.

As I returned to the room full of men, each of them watched me enter. Hiding my arousal was useless when they could easily smell my pheromones from the next room.

"Is everything all right?" asked Khalen.

"Fine. She's a bit miffed about the room arrangement is all."

Gabrihen scoffed. "Yeah, that sounds about right."

Connor raised his hands. "Well, I'm not bunkin' with her. That girl could freeze a fire from a mile away."

Khalen growled, his golden eyes focused on the careless young man.

"Sorry," Connor quickly and wisely countered. "I'm just saying—"

Gabrihen shoved him hard in the shoulder.

"The matter is not under discussion," I said. "The arrangement will remain."

Khalen studied me as I retook my place beside Teak. There was pride behind that stare, mixed with a bit of concern and question.

After taking a deep breath and a sip of his brandy, Khalen asked me, "You said that Steed had ulterior motives?"

"I believe so, yes."

"Come with me." He set his glass down before looking over at the tall man who closely resembled him in looks and stature. "You too, Seth."

As we followed him out of the room, I felt Teak's eyes upon me, probably wondering the same thing as me. *Stay here*, I told him telepathically. *I'll fill you in later.*

Khalen led us down the hall and into his chamber. Compared to the other rooms, this one was huge. A California King bed occupied the center of the room, covered by a cream-colored comforter. Two large armoires and a valet lined the far wall, while two recliners sat beneath the window. Dark burgundy velvet curtains hung from wrought iron rods, framing an amazing view of the snow-covered mountains. Another solid birch wood door led to what I assumed was the master bathroom.

Khalen then turned to face me, his golden eyes scanning me from head to toe. "You've been chipped."

"Another? How do you know?"

"It's one of my gifts," said Khalen.

One of many, I thought. The man had few limits and the power that radiated from him made his bones vibrate.

Seth stepped forward. "What do you see?"

"A chip, the size of a rice grain." He placed his hand

over my right shoulder blade. "Here."

I suddenly remembered an odd hum shortly preceding Steed's sudden retreat earlier that day. "Can this chip be read from a distance?"

"Possibly," said Seth, "but not likely. Most chips are designed to be read at close distance."

"But it is possible?" asked Khalen.

"Aye, it is. Why?"

Khalen began pacing, his brows knit in concentration. "Shifters, drugs, chips, Bennet Graves."

Seth and I remained silent, allowing the leader to process his thoughts, random as they might seem.

Khalen stopped pacing. "Seth, I need you to test Zebastian's blood."

"For what?" I asked.

"I think they were looking for you. Bennet wants you back."

I scoffed. "Why would they care about me when they have so many others who are far less trouble?"

"That's what I intend to find out. Bennet doesn't act on a whim. He wouldn't risk threatening my daughters without good reason."

Seth frowned in concentration, an uncanny resemblance to Khalen. "What, exactly, are you looking for?"

"Anomalies in the blood. Zebastian said they took his blood and offered him serum. There must be a reason."

Seth looked over at me. "Did they only use shifter blood?"

"Yes, as far as I could tell." The minds of these men worked so fast it was difficult to keep up. I heard the mental chatter between them, but it was too full of medical terms to keep pace.

Khalen must have sensed my confusion and graciously explained, "Seth discovered anomalies in Rae's blood and did some investigating. His mate is half Fae, making her blood slightly different than that of full Spirians. Seth has a theory that shifters come from Fae bloodlines."

I thought about their lost son, Zhentu, and how he was a shifter. "Are you or Skye part Fae, then?"

"No, but we believe that Skye's father, Shanuk, had some Fae in his bloodline, which explains why he was so powerful."

Seth shifted the conversation to something more pertinent. "There is a decent lab at the university. Can you get permission to use it?"

"Aye, I can. Tonight, however, we need to remove that chip."

That didn't sound good. "Tonight?"

He nodded, leaving little room for argument. Soon after he telepathically summoned Skye, she entered the room. Khalen gestured for me to take a seat in one of the chairs.

"Here?" I choked out, not sure I wanted someone digging around my shoulder for a grain-sized chip. Earlier, I learned that both of them were skilled surgeons so there was no concern about their abilities to do this properly. I just found it odd that they were doing it now, here in this room.

Khalen retrieved a black bag from a huge closet, opened it on the bed, and retrieved a needle and a small vile of fluid. With practiced ease, he drew the liquid out through the needle. "Remove your shirt."

I looked over at Seth who stood with confidence. As Khalen handed him plastic-wrapped implements, he placed them onto a stainless steel tray. Both of them donned pale-blue latex gloves.

Khalen pushed the air from the needle and vile. "This will sting a bit, but it will numb you enough to ease the pain. Skye will take care of the rest, while I remove the chip."

Feeling that this was a very bad idea, I removed my shirt and turned around. The sting of the needle was an afterthought compared to the thoughts bombarding my brain. As he administered the liquid around my shoulder blade, I couldn't help thinking about the times when I had endured severe torture at the hands of those SOAR Shadows. The memories caused my heart to race with adrenaline.

Skye rested her hands on my arm for reassurance. "Try to relax, Zebastian." When she saw me take a deep breath, she nodded to her mate.

I felt the pressure of the scalpel and warmth as blood trickled down my back. Seth expertly wiped it away, making sure to stay out of Khalen's way.

Next, I felt the forceps but no pain. I was sure Skye had something to do with that as well as the calm that blanketed my anxieties. The hum of her energy filled the room.

"Got it," said Khalen, dropping the chip into a small metal tin.

In less than a minute, my wound was healed by Skye. Seth finished cleaning me up, dumping the bloodied gauze into a plastic bag. The entire procedure looked very well-rehearsed. Standing, I donned my shirt. "You do this a lot, I take it?"

"It is occasionally necessary, yes," said Khalen, glancing over at Skye. After adding the soiled implements to the red plastic bio-hazard bag, he handed the cleaned chip to

Seth. "Hang on to that."

Moments later, Ian entered the room, obviously having been summoned by Khalen. "What did you find?"

Seth handed him the chip.

"Can you scan that?" asked Khalen.

"Not here, but Jackson, an old mucker of mine, has a clinic in town. I can see him tomorrow."

"Good," said Khalen. "I need to know what it reads as well as to whom it is registered."

"Every chip is registered to someone. If it were bought here in the States, Jackson will find the bloke who shelled for it."

Skye came up to me, placing her soft, gentle hand on my shoulder. "You okay?"

"Yeah." In truth, I was anything but okay, and I think she sensed it, having uncanny empathy to her spirit. I'd had a chip taken out of me that I never knew existed, and Khalen believed that Bennet wanted me back. If that were so, why did they go after Kaili? The whole thing left me feeling confused and somewhat alarmed. Was I endangering this clan? Were they now a target for Bennet and whatever he was planning?

"Get those thoughts out of your head, Zebastian," said Khalen. "They don't serve you and certainly not this clan."

"If Bennet wants me back, then my being here with you will place you and your clan in danger."

The leader turned to face me. "This feud between Bennet and I goes way back before you, Zebastian. He took my son. Finding you was a blessing—one that obviously has Bennet worried."

A blessing? Had I heard that right? His clan was in danger and I stood as the reason. How could that possibly be a blessing?

Khalen glanced around the room, and one by one, Ian, Seth, and Skye filed out, closing the door behind them. Khalen must have asked them to leave. He gestured toward the two chairs by the window. "Sit, Zebastian."

I did as he asked, feeling like a young child about to be scolded. It was difficult to feel otherwise in this man's presence. I couldn't help wonder whether I would have had the same presence one day if my father hadn't ostracized me from the clan. I had been raised to be a leader. Today, I wasn't sure what I would be.

"Your mind chatter is like that of a teenage girl," said Khalen. "Calm your thoughts or, one day, they will be your undoing."

I smiled, a weak attempt to look amused. "Most people cannot hear my thoughts."

He hooked a brow, not convinced. "Leaders can read you, Zebastian; have no doubt about that. You, too, will be a leader in this life. There is a strength about you that will not be denied."

I looked away, unable to meet his gaze. This man saw far too much for my comfort. "I have no clan."

"Untrue. You are part of my clan until you choose otherwise."

I hadn't been formally initiated into his clan. We were not connected, nor had I vowed fealty to him. Would I, if he asked it of me? For years I had been told stories of this man and had admired him from afar. Now, I served under him; a gift I wasn't sure I deserved.

He sighed. "Again, with the thoughts. Yes, it is true that we have not yet formally connected, but know this—you are under my charge and are part of this clan. Formalities can wait until you have made a decision."

"You don't know me, Khalen. I don't even know me. I do things—horrible things that I can't remember. Those Shadows changed me somehow. They turned me into a monster."

He sat beside me on the other chair, turning it to face me. "They changed you, yes, but not into a monster. I believe they altered your DNA, which is why I want Seth to test your blood."

"Why would they do that?"

"Bennet is building an army of super shifters, those with great power and strength."

I thought back to the night when Kaili was almost abducted. The shifter had infiltrated Khalen's wards as if they were no more than a standard shock. Most Spirians, shifter or no, would have died trying to enter that house uninvited. "Yes, perhaps you're right."

Khalen grew silent for a moment. "This, however, is not what I wanted to discuss with you."

I sat back, trying to pierce his thoughts, a ridiculous notion considering he was a leader with far more skill than I could ever dream of having.

That thought made him smile. "One day, Zebastian, your skills may surpass my own. Of this, I have no doubt."

I scoffed. "You see far too much in me, sir. It honors me that you do, but I don't believe it is justified."

"Some things happen whether we believe in them or not."

My thoughts shifted to Kaili, the spirited female I would have never approached voluntarily. She was definitely not my type. Yet somehow, she had weaseled her way into my heart and sparked every protective instinct I had to keep her safe and close. How, in God's world, had that happened?

Khalen smiled. "That is what I wanted to talk to you about."

I said nothing, waiting for him to explain.

"My daughter, Kaili."

"What about her?" The calmness I had tried to force into my voice sounded more like a bugle played by an amateur.

Khalen's expression fell as if what he had to say was painful, and perhaps a bit disheartening. "She is innocent, Zebastian."

I laughed. "Oh, Khalen, she is many things, but innocent is not one of them."

His golden eyes didn't waver. "She has never lain with a man."

I felt the blood drain from my face. I had kissed the female, fully expecting her to know how to react. I was forceful, dominant, insensitive—all the things a man should never be to an innocent female.

"Has your father talked to you about females?"

I knew what he was asking. When a man comes into his own, his father discusses the nuances of being a good male and how to care properly for a female. It is at that time when the father blesses his son with a mating pendant—the one he will, one day, give to his mate. "He never had a chance."

Khalen leaned forward in his chair, gripping me with those hypnotic eyes that mimicked the sun. "Kaili is interested in you, Zebastian. You are the first male she has ever shown any interest in at all."

Scoffing, I said, "She certainly has an odd way of showing it."

"I know I'm not your father, and I have no right to have this conversation with you, but I feel it is necessary."

The sincerity in his voice made my throat close with emotion. This talk was hard on him, not because of the subject matter, but because he felt it was not his place. He was doing something my father should have done. I opened my mouth to speak—to tell him all was well and I would be honored for him to explain the role of a Spirian male. It was one instinct that Spirians were not innately born with, which made the young dependent on the elders to shed some light. I was not exactly innocent, but this bonding added a new dimension to my attraction to Kaili; one I did not understand or could control.

"Will you let me pass on to you the role of a Spirian male?"

I nodded, still unable to speak. In a sense, the man was treating me as a son. It was akin to a human adopting a child. By Spirian law, he was asking to be my adoptive father.

"I am not properly prepared for this and will have to give you your pendant later. I must say, I was rather shocked at Kaili's response to you—I think we all were."

"The female wants nothing to do with me. You saw her reaction to the news that we were sharing a room."

"Aye, I did. She would not have reacted the same if it were anyone else."

"I guess I should feel honored, yes?"

He laughed. "Well, every other male who tried to kiss her ended up injured or worse. The fact that you were able to walk away from the experience should say something."

"I had to work for the honor, believe me. If I had allowed her to gain purchase of any measure, I too, would not be walking, let alone comfortably."

That earned a chuckle from the formidable leader. "Yes, she is one of Drew's most talented female students.

He is responsible for teaching our young men to fight, and he is very good at his job. I was against him teaching our females how to fight. Now you know why."

"It certainly weeds out males who are not strong enough to handle them."

"True enough," he laughed. His expression then turned serious again. "You and Kaili are a good match, but it must be her choice, agreed?"

"Of course, but I don't believe either one of us is ready to mate. I feel a strong bond to her, though."

"Aye, I've noticed. Your scent is all over her."

I had to smile at that thought. "I've heard of men bonding to their mates, but I never imagined it would happen to me at such a young age."

"Needless to say that it has, indeed, happened, and you must be prepared. The information I am about to share with you has been handed down through generations and is what you will pass down to your sons."

I nodded, accepting the responsibility. What happened afterward was indescribable and unexpected. The knowledge that passed from Khalen to me was nothing short of ethereal in nature and surreal in truth. In a matter of minutes, I had the knowledge to unite with a female, impregnate her, and to connect to her in spirit. I was also given the knowledge of how to end that bond—something I never wanted to consider, seeing that broken unions could only end in death.

"Uniting will not occur without ceremony. Understand?"

I nodded. "Understood."

"She will try to push you away, Zebastian. Do not allow her to do so."

"What if she means it?"

"She won't. You are what she needs and has wanted for a long time, and she knows that—to the point where it frightens her."

I studied the man for a while, wondering why he was trusting me with his daughter—with this knowledge.

He stood and patted me on the shoulder. "Intuition, Zebastian. Intuition."

Chapter 16

~ Kaili ~

ZE AND **FATHER** ENTERED THE dining room late. Every male in the room had his eyes trained on Ze as if he had sprouted wings or something. He did have a new look to him, though I couldn't say what it was other than a light that shone around him. He sat across from me as Father planted a long lingering kiss on Mum's lips before taking his place at the head of the table. Gabrihen, of course, had the right to the other end of the table, but he always gave it up to Aidan out of respect. I admired him for that. Now, if he could just treat his sisters with the same regard—fat chance of that happening.

Ze smiled over at me; an imp with a secret he wasn't about to share. I didn't care. He believed that we would talk about our room arrangement. He was sadly mistaken. After dinner, Shaiya and I were going to watch movies until we both passed out. That was the plan, anyway.

Gabrihen looked at me, then at Father, and finally at Ze. The slow smile that spread over his face was disturbing. As usual, he shielded his thoughts from me, a gift my father had bestowed upon him, I was sure. It seemed the sons of leaders acquired all the cool gifts, leaving us poor females to fend for ourselves. If it weren't for Mum's persistence, Shaiya and I would never have learned to defend ourselves with the help of Drew. He was a master at martial arts and hand-to-hand combat. I fully intended to demonstrate a few of those lessons to Ze, should he get any ideas about our so called room arrangement.

The dinner conversation was comprised of plans about some blood testing and such. Father had contacted his friend at the university to arrange some time in the lab, and to ensure that Shaiya and I could take our test.

"Shaiya, Kaili," said Father, "you take your finals tomorrow."

I nearly choked on the flavorful meat sauce that accompanied an ample portion of angel hair pasta. The sauce alone was a meal in itself; thick, tangy, and filled with veggies and ground elk meat. It was a shame I had lost my appetite for it now. "Tomorrow?"

"Aye. It is the only day available when you will have protection."

"Father, I have five classes. I cannot possibly study for all of them in one evening."

He took a sip of his wine before responding with a cold and calloused, "Find a way, Kaili. There are no other options."

"I'll help you," said Shaiya, daintily dabbing her mouth with the red cloth napkin. "My only final is for choreography, and that will be a cinch."

"What about your performance?"

"With numb-nuts, really? Ya think that's a loss?"

I frowned, confused by how easily Shaiya could forego an entire semester of dance; she practically lived to perform. "Yes, it is a loss, Shaiya. You've worked hard for this role. It's important to you."

"There will be other roles, Kaili, and better dance partners. Shelby has been vying for my part for the past three months. She'll be thrilled if I don't show up, believe me."

All I could do was look at her and shake my head like some clueless blonde in a windstorm. Was I the only one miffed about this? Sipping my wine, I thought about how I was going to pass those finals. I knew my stuff, that was a given, and I had a photographic memory like my Uncle Seth, but still. Taking five finals in one day was taxing for anyone, gifts or no. So much for watching movies all night.

Conversations continued to hum around the sturdy rosewood table. I pushed the pasta around on my plate, hoping my appetite would return.

"Are you not likin' your meal, miss?" asked Tisha, the kind old caretaker of the cabin. She wore her auburn hair in a tightly coiled bun. The apron she had on was white with pink embroidery that formed wildflowers over the front. Beneath she wore blue jeans and a cotton tee-shirt, simple, yet practical. Father allowed her to live here free in exchange for her services during our stays. She genuinely enjoyed cooking for us and ensuring the place was clean and well-stocked. Her husband traveled a lot, leaving her here alone too often. She was human, but knew about our kind, though she had not quite grown used to the constant headaches that accompanied our presence. Mum helped remove the pain, but she had to do it often.

"I'm fine, Tisha. The meal is one of my favorites."

She gestured to my plate. "But you don't eat."

Ze reached over to take my plate. "I'll eat it for her."

I stabbed his hand with my fork. The plate dropped from his hand as he pulled it back with a hushed curse.

"Bloody hell, Kaili; what was that for?"

"Taking my plate. What do you think?"

"You're not eating it. The food is going to waste."

I wrapped a huge wad of angel hair onto my fork and stuffed it into my mouth.

"Kaili!" Mum blurted. "Where are your manners?"

I was very tempted to answer her with a mouth full of macerated pasta, but Father was already glaring and I didn't want to feel his wrath. Swallowing, I followed the oversized portion with a swig of wine. "Sorry, Mum."

Shaiya nudged me. "What's up with you?"

"Just a bit amped up, that's all." I avoided looking across the table at Ze. He was staring at me; I could feel it. His thoughts were closed, not that I was interested.

"Relax," she said. "You know your stuff. The finals will be a snap. They always are for you."

Damn it, he was still staring. I glanced up at him. "You're being rude."

He chuckled, laying down a chunk of bread he had been eating. "And you're the epitome of manners, yeah?"

"You tried to take my meal."

"You weren't eating it. I didn't want it to go to waste and hurt poor Tisha's feelings."

I narrowed my eyes at him, wishing I had the power to shoot laser beams from my pupils, disintegrating my enemies. Tiny red pricks dappled his hand where I had stuck him with my fork. I gestured toward it. "Does that hurt?"

He glanced down at his hand. "No, but thank you for asking." Wrong answer, I thought, already strategizing another way in which to make my point clear to him that

I was not happy about him taking liberties with my room.

"I'm very aware of your feelings," he chided, smiling and digging into a third portion of spaghetti. Tisha, having been charmed by his comments, gave him three huge meatballs on top, with extra cheese.

He took another bite of bread, washing it down with a few sips of water. I rarely saw him drink anything but water, and I found that rather odd. Looking around the table, every male had some sort of alcoholic beverage, be it wine, scotch, or brandy. Teak, too, drank water, probably to be like his friend.

He and Ze exchanged glances before Ze explained, "Shifters don't do well with alcohol. It's best if they don't consume it at all."

"Why's that?" asked Shaiya.

The conversations at the table quieted, indicating that there was more than her interest at stake here.

It was Teak who answered. "Shifters, by nature, are a moody bunch, much like their shifter animals—dangerous and unpredictable."

"But alcohol doesn't affect Spirians," said Shaiya.

"Alcohol does not affect Spirians as it does humans, but it still affects us in other ways. After drinking, it is far more difficult for a shifter to maintain control. If riled, we could end up hurting someone."

Was Shaiya actually blushing? I had never seen her blush in the presence of a male—ever.

Teak noticed the color as well and offered a smile in return. Good grief. The entire exchange was enough to kill my appetite forever. I pushed my plate away. "Father, may I be excused to study?"

As expected, he did not miss the exchange between us all. He nodded.

Tisha came in to collect my plate. "Should I have dessert sent up to you?"

"That would be lovely, Tisha; thank you." With that, I scooted my chair out, folded my napkin, and left without sparing anyone but Father and Mum a glance.

I heard Ian laugh. "That girl's spirit grows feistier with each passin' year, yeah?"

Gabrihen scoffed. "You got that right. What she needs is to get la—"

Father cleared his throat. "Enough!"

The conversation came to a screeching halt. Wanting to disappear out of the house and just keep going, I eyed the front door. Bad idea, I thought. Father would tan my hide and then some if I did something that stupid. It was best just to go upstairs and study my brains out until sunrise. Tomorrow was going to be a very long day.

THREE HOURS LATER, AND FOUR books spent, I was ready for a break. As if on cue, a knock sounded upon the door. I assumed it was dear Tisha, bringing me dessert and hopefully a steamy cup of Lady Grey tea. "Come in."

A tray landed upon the desk, bearing two plates of blackberry cobbler and two cups of tea.

"Ah, you're an angel," I chimed.

"Why, thank you. Coming from that mouth, it's quite a compliment."

I looked up into deep gray eyes that could melt an iceberg in winter. "I didn't know it was you," I seethed.

Scoffing, he began pouring cream into one of the cups of tea. "From sweet to bitter in two seconds—impressive." He added a bit of honey and stirred before placing the cup before me. Without invitation, he pulled a chair over and sat facing me.

"How do you know how I take my tea?"

"Your thoughts are clear as rain to me, even when you don't want them to be."

I sipped the tea that was perfectly treated. I wouldn't tell him that though. "Care to tell me how you manage to do that, seeing you aren't a male of this clan?" The last part came out a bit harsh, but tonight, I just didn't care. My attitude was beyond filtering. At this point, it needed a full-blown renovation.

My jibe didn't affect him in the least. He just sipped his black tea as if it were fine aged brandy. "I'm not sure. I cannot do it with everyone—just you."

"Hmm, lucky me."

The cobbler was still warm and spiced with cinnamon and cardamom. A fluffy puff of whipped cream topped the thing and was sprinkled with dark chocolate flakes. By the time I took my first tangy bite, Ze had nearly polished off half of his dessert. The man had an appetite for certain. Funny how that could be a turn on. Like he needed more help in that department. The male was all muscle and attitude and someone I couldn't best—damn him.

A smile crept over those annoyingly seductive lips. "How's the studying going?"

I glanced over at the four spent books, and then over at the other ten still waiting for my attention. "Peachy. I figure in about another eight hours or so, I'll be ready."

He finished his dessert, placing the plate back onto the tray. When his hungry gaze fell over to my plate, I pulled it toward my stomach.

"Need any help?"

"No. Go shoot pool with the men, or do whatever it is you guys do at night."

I heard Shaiya giggle as she and Teak went into her room. Rolling my eyes, I took a sizable bite of my cobbler, not really caring how unladylike it seemed. "My sister likes your friend."

He shrugged. "Mutual attractions are not uncommon between young Spirians."

Unless you were me, I thought.

"Why the sudden frown, Kaili?"

God, his voice could soothe a hurricane. Taking a deep breath, I forced my face to look indifferent. All that did was make him laugh.

"You're very cute, you know that?" When he reached for me, I leaned back and quickly stuffed my face with another bite—my last.

"More?"

I shook my head, placing the empty plate onto the tray. "I need to get back to work."

He sat back, sipping his tea as if challenging me to make him leave. It didn't help that Shaiya and Teak were doing God only knew what next door. They certainly weren't being quiet about it.

"Why does your sister sharing affections with a male bother you so much?"

Blood flooded my face. "It doesn't."

The hook of his brow indicated disbelief. He stood and collected the tray. "I'll give you two more hours, and then we will talk."

"I won't be done in two hours."

Without a word, he walked out, taking the tray with him. The man was infuriating.

Chapter 17

~Zebastian~

THE FEMALE ACTUALLY BLUSHED OVER the fact that her sister and Teak were sharing affections in the adjoining room. I found that fact intriguing and disturbing. Affections between Spirians were always something that was encouraged in the young. It was never something to be ashamed of or accompanied by guilt. When I had asked her about it, her thoughts turned to a wall of impenetrable steel. What would cause such a reaction? I wondered.

Entering the kitchen, I nearly ran into Tisha as she rushed to clean the evening's mess. She brought her tiny hand up to her ample chest and heaved in a breath.

"Goodness, Zebastian; ye nearly had me soil m'self."

"Sorry, Tisha. I was just bringing this back to you. Did you need help with all this?" I gestured to the massive kitchen counters littered with dirty pans and dishes.

"Oh, no, dear boy. I must earn my keep in this lovely place, and Master Khalen is very generous as it is."

"Two pairs of hands make quick work, and besides, I

could use a female to talk to."

Her expression fell to one that my mother would sport whenever I came to her with a problem. "Do ye now?"

I filled the sink with soapy water and added a stack of plates to soak. "Tell me something. What would cause a female to be embarrassed about sharing affections?"

"Are we talkin' about young Kaili?"

"We are."

She set another stack of plates beside me and opened one of the many dishwashers for me to load. "She's an innocent, Zebastian. From what little I know of the Spirian race, this is akin to being giftless, is it not?"

"Her reaction is not just that of an innocent. It runs deeper than that."

Tisha worked the other sink and dishwasher, her efficiency in the kitchen evident. "Have ye thought of askin' her?"

I felt my jaw tighten and flex. "Yes, and she closed up tight as a steel drum."

"And this bothers you?"

A question that didn't merit an answer, which caused Tisha to tick her tongue. "Ah, the mysteries of a woman in the heart of a man."

I loaded the last plate from the sink before reaching for another stack. "Meaning?"

"Men always want to fix a woman's problems. Sometimes, those problems don't want to be fixed; they just want to be acknowledged."

Okay, perhaps this was a mistake. My confusion was growing foggier by the minute. "Acknowledged?"

"Aye. Listen to her lad, without trying to fix every issue she reveals. When she's ready, she'll talk, and if she doesn't, she'll show you in her actions."

I continued to work, shaking my head. "Why do females make everything so bloody complicated?"

Another person entered the room, her steps so quiet they were barely detectible. "Because," said Skye, "if we were easy, you males would lose interest."

Khalen lifted her up from behind and swung her around. "Don't count on it. A little easiness would be very much appreciated at times."

"Amen," I chimed in.

Skye giggled like a young girl. When I glanced over, Khalen had her cradled in his arms, covering her with kisses. My parents were affectionate with each other like that. My heart ached with the thought of them. Had they missed me? Mother looked so heartbroken with Father's decision. The pain in her eyes still flashed clear as day in my mind's eye. It was the last thing I remembered before Teak whisked me away.

I returned my thoughts to the task at hand. It didn't take long for them to wander to the unruly blonde waiting in our room. Introducing her to the way of sex was going to be tricky. The only females I had experience with were trained Shadow slaves who did what they were told. Shifter males were forced to take them to protect our sanity as well as to entertain the Shadows—sick bastards.

Khalen wanted me to take her innocence. It was an honor to be asked and one that I would not squander. Not to mention, the mere thought that another male would eventually have her made my blood boil.

Having finished loading the machine, I set it to cycle. Before seeing the fiery female, I would need to run off some of this energy. Without a word, I headed toward the back door, shifted to my wolf and ran.

Shifter

~Kaili~

I HEARD THE BACK DOOR slam and immediately felt Ze's anxiety and power as he ran through the brush and into the adjoining woods. My heart pumped in cadence with his, my lungs filling with breath, cold, and damp. The scent of pine and maple was thick, along with the scent of deer and vermin. The forest was full of life, and experiencing it through Ze's senses made it all the more powerful.

Pushing my book aside, I closed my eyes and reveled in the gift that was Ze's. What would it be like to shift? I wondered. I reached out to feel more of him, the earth beneath his paws, the coldness in his fur.

Enjoying the ride? he asked in thought, snapping me back to my stuffy room and the ambient murmurs coming from the movie playing in Shaiya's room. Teak was still with her. After having been at it for what seemed like hours, they were finally taking a break—thank God.

I heard Ze's laughter, or was it his wolf's. Wolves didn't laugh, did they? Again, the chortle rattled my mind. *Do you mind?* I seethed.

Not at all, he replied.

I slammed closed my book and stacked it on top of the others. My mind was spent and my body felt like a knot that had been wound far too tight. A hot bath sounded perfect. I gathered a few things and a pair of soft P.J.'s before padding my way to the bathroom.

The sunken tub surrounded by Jerusalem tile welcomed me like an old friend. I closed the door, set my things down, and then proceeded to light the plethora of scented candles that surrounded the room—my mum's idea, and I loved her for it. Soft, mint green rugs softened the heated tile floors and felt good between my tired toes. After being scrunched under my chair, they felt cramped and weary.

As I began disrobing, part of me envied Ze and the way he could shift on the fly, running without a stitch of clothing. How freeing that must seem. I turned the water to hot and then adjusted the temperature as the tub began to fill. Not willing to wait, I stepped inside, sinking down until my back rested against the sloped side. I twisted my hair up and secured it in a bun on top of my head. Closing my eyes, I escaped to the sound of rushing water, warmth, and the lilac scented glow of the candles.

The peace didn't last long, though. My mind twisted with the echoes of my sister's pleasure, and then a memory of years long past. The image of Richard, a young Spirian male, manifested in full focus with his deep green eyes, black hair, and chiseled features that would make any female swoon. I remembered his kiss, his touch, and how I had wanted him so badly my belly clenched at the thought. When he discovered I was innocent, however, his passion and desires quickly turned to disgust. The rejection hurt so deeply, I'd sworn I'd never subject myself to that ever again. It was supposed to be an honor to be a female's first lover—an honor, not something to merit disgust. He said he wanted a female who knew what she was doing, not some innocent child looking for her first experience.

My breath caught in my throat as I stifled the emotions the memory invoked. Shaiya's first experience had been magical, or so she said. After Richard dumped me, I developed a reputation of being a cold-hearted spinster, untouched by anyone. For a while, males seemed to make it their personal challenge to break through my icy barrier, only succeeding in making it stronger and thicker than even I could manage.

I reached over and turned the faucet off, sinking back into the water and sighing. Would I die innocent? I thought. Was there anyone who would ever want me? Ze acted like he did, but that was just a game to him, like it was with every other male I encountered. The thought of him trying, however, sparked feelings in me that were new and strange. His kiss made me feel this way. A smile curled my lips. Ze had kissed me and it was wonderful.

An hour passed before I padded my way back to the room. The lights were turned off. When I clicked them back on, I saw Ze sitting on his bed, legs crossed, eyes closed, and shirtless. At least he had the decency to don a pair of jeans.

Quietly, I put my clothes away, turned off the light, and tiptoed to my bed. Trying not to make a noise, I turned down my covers and crawled under them.

"Enjoy your bath?" he asked, his voice deep and a bit groggy.

"Yes, thank you."

"So, tell me more about this Richard character."

My face paled as my blood retreated back to my overprotective heart. "Richard?" my voice cracked.

"Yes, the idiot who refused to have first rights with you."

Damn his thought intrusions. Was nothing sacred to him?

"He was an idiot; you do realize that, yes?"

"Stay out of my thoughts, Zebastian."

He stood from his bed and turned on the lights. He then closed the door and strode toward me like a man with a mission. It was slightly alarming. Instinctively, I scooted back against the wall.

"Talk to me, Kaili, or risk taking those finals without a wink of sleep."

"Don't do this to me, Ze. Please, I beg of you."

"Talk."

Biting my lower lip, I forced my tongue to work. "Yes, he was an idiot."

His eyes narrowed to blue slivers, glowing like the sea under moonlight. "Your words, but not your thoughts. He made you feel dirty, didn't he?"

"Does it matter?"

He sat beside me, making an effort to touch me. I scooted away from him. This, of course, was like playing keep away from a dog that lived for the game of tug-of-war. With impressive speed, he grabbed me and pulled me onto his lap. Knowing full well that I would retaliate, he captured my arms and pinned my flailing legs with one of his own.

"Relax," he growled. "I just want to talk."

"Let me go."

"No."

I struggled against him until my energy was spent and my emotions were raw. Unable to hold them back any longer, tears flooded my eyes and I wept for the first time in many years. He just held me, allowing me to purge the shame and anger from my heart and mind. I cried like an injured child in his arms.

Just when I thought I could control my pitiful emotions, another wave hit hard and deep, peeling away the wall that protected my heart. It would take nothing to tear it to pieces now—absolutely nothing.

Ze rocked me, kissing the top of my head as if I were something precious. I wasn't though, was I? A victorious challenge was what I had become, nothing more.

"Happy now?" I croaked between gut-wracking sobs. "Congratulations. You got the ice queen to cry."

"I want you to talk to me and tell me what he said to you. If that means waiting through this emotional outpour, then so be it."

"Read my thoughts, Zebastian. You seem to be quite adept at it."

"I want to hear the words from your lips."

Again, I tried to break free. His damn grip was like iron bands. I tried every trick Drew had shown me for breaking out of a hold. Nothing phased the man. I pinched the tender skin under his arm, jabbed my elbow into his ribs. He didn't even flinch. I even pressed my elbow into the top of his thigh—nothing. Was the man numb?

"I feel the pain you are inflicting, I assure you," he said, his voice alarmingly calm. "I've just been trained to ignore it."

"You can't ignore it forever." With that, I pinched as hard as I could. Now he had my hands pinned as well.

"Fight me all you want, Kaili. It won't do you any good."

"I can call my father up here. I don't believe he will be pleased with your handling of me."

"By all means. Call him."

Remembering what Drew had said about the relax reflex, I stopped my struggles and grew limp in Ze's arms. "Okay, you win. I'll talk."

His grip loosened, but he was still in control. I needed him distracted. "Can you just hold me, please?"

"I am holding you, Kaili."

"I mean hug me," I said in the sweetest voice I could muster.

"I take it you're done crying then?"

Cold-hearted bastard. Gritting my teeth, I told myself to stay calm and sweet. "Not yet. I just want you to hold me—nicely."

"You're far too trusting. I think I like you just like this."

Calm, I silently thought. Stay calm. Deep down, however, I wanted to neuter the bugger. The anger ruling my thoughts made it impossible to fake sobs with any measure of believability. We were now at a stalemate. "Let me go and I'll talk."

"Your word?"

Through gritted teeth, I growled, "My word."

He lifted me with far too much ease and set me down beside him, making sure my body was wedged between him and the wall.

"Whatever you're thinking, Kaili, stop now. I'll know what you're going to do before you even try it. Now, you gave me your word. Stay true to it or I will bend you over my lap and—"

I held up my hand, not wanting to hear what horrid thing he wanted to do to me. "Okay, okay. You win. I'll spill."

He turned to face me, opening a nice shot to his tender region. If I were quick, he would not have time to react.

A low growl vibrated in his throat. "Stop scheming and start talking."

Closing my eyes, I shook my head. This was an impossible situation, one I would bring up to Drew as soon as we returned home. "Fine. Richard said he wanted a female who knew what she was doing, not some innocent child looking for her first experience." Glaring at him, I added, "Happy now?"

"And how did that make you feel?"

Shocked that he would even ask such an inane question, I opened my mouth to answer, but nothing came out.

"Angry, hurt?" he prompted.

"Yes, of course. Who wouldn't feel those things?"

"Say it. Tell me how you felt."

I thought about calling my father, but his blasted ability to read intentions would backfire on me. "Angry," I blurted, "confused, hurt, embarrassed, shamed, jealous, envious—inadequate."

"Good."

Without thought, I flipped back and fully intended to nail the insensitive jerk in his arrogant thick head. He grabbed my legs and had me pinned beneath him so quickly that I barely had time to take my next breath.

"You very much challenge my control, Kaili. Be warned; I haven't much left."

"You got what you wanted from me, Ze; now let me go. Please; I'm very tired, and I'm done fighting you."

"Who were you jealous and envious of?"

I shook my head. "What?"

"You said you felt jealous and envious."

"Among other things."

"Of whom?"

I was beyond tired, and he was tearing down my defenses faster than I could reconstruct them. Weary, I said, "Shaiya."

"Why?"

"I'm done talking."

"No, you're not. Why were you jealous and envious of your twin?"

"Because, she is better in bed than I am. She has no issues getting men and making them happy. She makes it look easy and even enjoyable."

"And you feel that you cannot please a man in bed?"

"I'm the ice queen, remember? How pleasurable can that be?"

"You weren't an ice queen when I kissed you."

"I faked it—to get you to stop."

The fall of his expression felt like a dagger to my heart. His grip on me eased.

"You found your calling. Join the drama club because you sure had me fooled." He slid away from me and returned to his bed.

"Look," I said. "I'm sorry. Something in me is broken and I don't know how to fix it."

"Sometimes things don't need to be fixed; they just need to be acknowledged." He walked over and turned out the light. "Goodnight, Kaili." Pain deepened his voice—laced with defeat.

Chapter 18

~Zebastian~

TEAK NUDGED MY SHOULDER AS we waited for Seth to prepare the blood draw. "What has you in such a foul mood?"

"I'm done with this gig, Teak. I want to find that shifter son of Khalen's and get the hell out of this country."

"Rough night?"

That earned him a growl. "Be careful, my friend. You are treading on fragile ground."

Seth returned with twelve vials, a long rubber flat band, and a needle that made Polish sausage look thin. "Ready?"

I rolled up my sleeve. As he tourneyed my arm and searched for an adequate vein, his brows furrowed, shadowing his golden eyes.

"There's a lot of scar tissue in here."

"That happens when you're used as a test subject for twelve years."

The shadows over his eyes deepened. "Twelve years?"

"Yep," I answered unenthusiastically.

He found a suitable vein and then inserted the needle with practiced ease. As the first vial began to fill, he released the tourniquet and assembly-lined the remaining tubes.

"Okay," he said, removing the needle. "You're good to go."

"Sure you don't want tissue samples as well?" I asked in jest.

He reached over and plucked a strand of hair from my head. "No, this should suffice." He stuffed the short hair into a small sealable bag.

"Come on," I said to Teak. "Let's look for those Shadow bastards."

Seth, standing at a high counter, looked over his shoulder. "Khalen asked that you join him in the Red Square."

"Perfect," I muttered. "So much for getting anything done."

"You need an attitude adjustment, my friend." Teak opened the door, waiting for me to pass.

We walked to the Red Square in silence, which was just fine for me. I really wasn't in the mood to listen to Teak's ramblings about what a great night he had, and how sweet Shaiya was opposed to her twin. The thoughts in his mind were bad enough. No wonder he was in such a good mood.

As we approached Khalen, a familiar scent lingered in the air. I scanned the area, but the scent did not intensify from any direction. Steed had to be near. I held my finger up to Khalen, indicating that he should wait before speaking. He, too, looked around, seeking the danger that had me alarmed. I sent him an image of Steed. He nodded.

"Shift," I told Teak, preparing to do the same thing.

His eagle bounced out of the fallen clothes and took flight. My wolf detected Steed's scent fading quickly. He had been cloaking his presence in an illusion. Teak reported seeing five Shadows, none of whom was Steed. Where was the bugger? Following my nose, I trotted East, Khalen following close behind after collecting our clothes.

I tried communicating with the leader, but unlike Kaili, he didn't comprehend my wolf's thoughts. God, the memory of her made my gut twist. I knew what she had said last night was a lie. What disturbed me further was that she had said it at all. She apologized, yes, but what for—hurting me with the truth or lying to me? I should have taken her and curbed this yearning. My body merely craved for what it was denied too long, nothing more.

My hackles stood on end, detecting danger. I stopped, scenting the air. Something was wrong. *Teak, what do you see?*

No response. *Teak!* I waited. He did not respond.

Khalen gestured toward the greenbelt darkened with trees. Using sign language, he suggested that it might be a trap. He might be right. I continued to summon Teak, trying to probe his thoughts. The silence sickened me. Had something happened to him?

Khalen and I approached the woods, listening and keeping our senses sharp. A Shadow came straight toward Khalen, but he didn't notice him. I lunged ahead of the leader, knocking the Shadow back. He countered with a blow to my head, but it felt more like a slap. I bit his hand before tearing out his throat.

They're cloaked, I tried to warn him, but he didn't understand. Three more Shadows approached. I growled three times, pointing my snout to the East. Khalen nodded.

The attack happened quickly. Khalen downed two of the men without even touching them. I knew he was a reaper, but seeing that gift in action was striking. I remembered seeing something similar when I escaped from the SOAR mansion. Had there been a reaper there that day? I didn't remember seeing anyone. Then again, I didn't remember much of anything from that day.

The third man came at me with two clubs connected by a six-inch chain. He was good with the thing, landing a few blows to my kidneys and ribs. I heard a rib snap and felt the sharp pain rip through my side. Khalen grabbed him, tossed him to the ground, and then quickly snapped his neck.

That was the last of them. The only scent I followed now was that of blood. Thirty feet away, a naked body lay in the midst of leaves and dirt. It was Teak. I shifted back into human form and leaned over his body. Khalen pressed his fingers against his throat, checking for a pulse. He pulled out his phone, making a call.

"Gabrihen, bring your mum—now!"

He placed the thing back into his pocket, then applied pressure to the deepest wound in his side. "Press that one there," he instructed, gesturing to the gash in Teak's leg. The blood, warm, thick, and wet, seeped through my fingers.

Gabrihen and Skye poofed into the woods only twenty feet away. She fell to her knees and purged her stomach before rushing toward us.

"What happened?" she asked, placing her hands on my friend.

"We were attacked," Khalen answered, his voice

sounding off. He tossed me the clothes he had gathered so I could get dressed.

She looked at her mate as if she could see him. "You're weak. How many did you reap?"

He sat down, looking as if he had witnessed his best friend stealing money. "Only two. It shouldn't be affecting me this way. They were only ... pawns." His face paled before he collapsed onto the ground.

"Father!" Gabrihen cried.

Skye pulled one hand off Teak and placed it onto her mate.

"Who's watching the girls?" I asked Gabrihen.

"Ian and Aidan have already taken them back to the cabin. Seth texted us. He's on his way as well. It's just us here."

When Teak started to stir, Skye pulled her hand away and focused her attention on Khalen. "Gabrihen, take Teak back with you, and then come back for your father."

"No," Khalen growled. "I'm fine."

Skye's lips grew firm as if biting back an argument. "Go," she said to Gabrihen. "We'll get him home."

Gabrihen looked down at his father, hesitant to leave.

"Do as she says, Son. I'll be all right."

I helped him lift Teak, and then poof, they were gone. The bigger trick would be getting Khalen and his blind mate back to the truck. These woods were thick with undergrowth. Carrying them both out of here made the most sense, but Khalen would never agree to that. I reached down to help him stand, grateful that he took the help.

"What the hell were those things?" he asked, struggling to stand.

"Like Steed, they work for SOAR, though they're not

tight like clanmates."

"They had the strength of leaders. Ordinary blokes wouldn't have affected me after reaping them."

"I don't believe they were ordinary. When Teak and I saw them going after Kaili, they were able to cast an illusion."

"That doesn't seem out of the ordinary. There are many illusionists among the Shadows, but even they don't have the kind of strength these boys showed."

"Illusions don't work on shifters. Theirs did."

"Let's hope Seth was able to find something useful in your samples." Khalen took a few steps on shaky legs. When I reached for his mate, he growled like an overprotective beast.

Skye rolled her eyes and moved over to Khalen's left side.

"You support him on the right, I'll handle the left."

Interesting plan seeing as she was several inches shorter than Khalen and at least fifty pounds lighter. Not wanting her to feel useless, I took the majority of the leader's weight. The relief was knowing she had something solid to hold on to should she trip over a log or something.

She negotiated the debris with practiced ease, making me wonder whether she really was blind after all.

"Just don't let her drive," said Khalen, having read my thoughts, "even if she claims she can."

"I can," she stated with confidence.

"That's a scary thought," I said.

W E RETURNED HOME JUST IN time for dinner. Not feeling up to eating at the table, I asked to have my meal in the privacy of my room. I was dirty, tired, and not in the mood for Kaili's attitude—not tonight.

A quick check on Teak to ensure he was on the mend, and I was good for a little quiet time. Leaving the meal in the room, I took a long shower and dressed into a pair of sweats that Gabrihen loaned me. I made quick work of the roast beef and mashed potatoes, before contemplating a run in the woods. I was exhausted, yet my mind was racing a thousand miles a minute.

A knock sounded on the door. I looked up to see Seth standing there, a grim look on his face. "May we enter?"

We? "Sure."

I sat upright in bed. Seth entered with Khalen. They pulled up a couple of chairs and sat down.

"Is everything all right?" I asked.

Seth spoke first. "You said that SOAR had been injecting you with serum?"

I nodded.

"How often?"

"Every day. Why?"

He and Khalen exchanged glances. "Your blood shows a dominating factor of Fae DNA."

I swung my legs over the side of the bed and placed my feet on the floor, needing to feel something solid. "What does that mean, exactly?"

Now it was Khalen's turn to talk. "You said they invoked your anger."

"Yeah."

"You also said that you blackout when your rage kicks in."

Again, "Yeah."

More glances exchanged between them.

"Care to share those thoughts?" I asked, not even trying to hide the anger in my voice.

Khalen studied me too intently for my comfort. "Bennet is building an army of super shifters."

"As you had suspected?"

"It explains the strength I sense in you and why those Shadows I reaped nearly drained me of energy."

My mind reeled with thoughts, like a torturous film designed to brainwash its viewer. Images of the dead men who surrounded me after my escape, the shifter who broke through Khalen's wards, the illusionists, flashed in my mind in a vivid collage.

"Zebastian?"

"It makes sense," I said. "Except for the attack today. That makes no sense at all."

Both men looked at me, waiting for more.

"The girls were protected by Ian and Aidan. Steed knew I could scent him. He drew us into those woods. Why?"

"To get to you," said Khalen. "They want you back. Injuring Teak was a surefire way to predict your location."

"They had to have known you were with me. The ambush was a risk."

"Aye, one that backfired."

"What if they had succeeded, though?" said Seth. "Khalen would have been incapacitated with exhaustion, and they would have you back. Teak was expendable. They wanted him to die, which is why they sliced his leg and side. If they brought you and Khalen to Bennet, imagine the reward."

"Why me? I gave them nothing but trouble."

"A few more doses of serum and they would be able to control your mind completely," Seth explained. "Without more of it, you would go insane. Thank God you escaped when you did."

I scoffed. "Hell, I'm halfway there as it is."

"We're gonna need help," said Khalen. "My clans can handle a Shadow attack, but a band of these super shifters will leave a destructive wake that will be hard, if not impossible, to recover from."

Both of them looked at me as if I had an answer. "What?"

"Your father is quite prevalent in the Northern territories, is he not?" asked Khalen.

"He is."

"If he gathered his clans, we could pose a formidable threat."

I took a deep breath, seeing my life slide away like the ocean tides. "And you want me to ask him?"

"I do."

"As an outcast, I enter his territories as a threat. I will be killed for trespassing without notice."

"I will contact him first and tell him I have sent you."

Facing my father again was like looking into the face of death ... not something I wanted or needed right now. "You ask a lot from me."

Khalen stood. "No more than you can handle." He patted my shoulder with his heavy hand.

Chapter 19

~Kaili~

Zebastian's insistent avoidance of me grated on my nerves. I knew what I said had hurt him, but dang, was he going to avoid me forever? I inwardly laughed at that. A week ago, I would have counted his absence as a blessing. For the past three days, though, I had barely caught a glimpse of him and he hadn't slept in our room. This morning, his clothes were gone. The shock of it sent my adrenaline pumping. Had he left for good?

Teak trotted down the stairs after spending some time with Shaiya. She was always happy, but somehow, Teak made her more so. Part of me was very jealous, but deep down, I knew this emptiness was all my doing. Zebastian had tried to tear down my defenses and I had attacked him like some vicious dog.

"Hi, Teak."

His smile broadened. "Hey, Kaili."

"Have you seen Ze?"

"Not since yesterday. He's been a bit of a recluse."

"Yeah, I've noticed. Well, if you see him, can you tell him we need to talk?"

He studied me for a moment. "Is everything all right?"

"Yeah, I just need to apologize to him; that's all."

Teak's expression grew solemn. "Reach out to him, Kaili. He's always been able to hear your thoughts."

I had thought so too, but lately, he hadn't responded to any of them, even my sweetest ones. "Yeah, good idea."

Teak walked over to me and placed his hand under my chin. "Don't just talk to him, Kaili. Tell him how you feel. Truth is important to Ze. Be honest. That's all he wants."

I nodded. "Okay ... thanks."

"You bet." He continued toward the kitchen.

A walk in the woods sounded perfect, perhaps even a swim in the lake. I loved to swim and missed my favorite spot back home. It would be cold, but that was what I wanted now—something cold and refreshing. I grabbed my coat and headed out the door.

The sweet scent of new maple leaves and fresh pine was like a slice of home. Subtle sounds of nature played in the background like a soft orchestra during a contemplative scene in a movie. Dried pine needles crunched beneath my feet as I followed the familiar path through Douglass fir, hemlock, and cedar. Small, bright green patches of wood sorrel grew in colonies under the bows of two-hundred-year-old trees. Snagging a few, I popped them into my mouth and enjoyed their sour flavor. Mum had introduced me to them when I was about five. I had loved them ever since.

Shaiya didn't share our love for nature. She was more of a city girl, enjoying the night life, dancing, and the loud expression of music. In many respects, she and I were like night and day. It was hard to believe we came from the same egg.

I rounded the corner, my eye catching the sight of

sleek golden fur on a white-tailed deer, startled by my approach. She bounded through the forest on legs that propelled her like springs over the thick brush and fallen trees. In a beat, she was gone and I was alone once again. The cool air felt sharp against my lungs. Being stuck in that cabin was beginning to make me crazy. It felt good to be outside and alone with my thoughts.

The lake glistened up ahead, its surface smooth as glass. Finding a large rock on which to lay my clothes, I removed them, biting back the cold stinging my skin. It was late spring, but still; the air had a bite to it as if trying to hold on to the last hours of winter. I stepped into the water, sending ripples out toward the center of the large lake. When I was hip deep, I took a long breath and dove beneath the surface. I had always been able to hold my breath for minutes at a time. It came naturally to me and I felt at peace in the water. Still too cold for plants to spring to life, the lakebed was bare, with only rocks and fine dirt to break up the flatness.

Underwater springs fed this lake so fish were non-existent here. Small pollywogs, frogs, and a few worms were all I saw. I surfaced somewhere near the center of the lake, having swam quite a distance. Rolling over onto my back, I took my time catching my breath before going down for another look.

Sensing something watching me, I looked over and saw Ze in his wolf form—large, gray and black fur, and eyes that looked like a midnight sky. If I didn't know him better, I could easily have thought he was there to eat me upon my exit. Seeing it was the only shore along the lake, I had no choice but to leave the way I came in.

Come out before you freeze to death, he said in thought. They were the first words he spoke to me in three days, and they were music to my heart.

Why don't you join me, instead?

I could feel his growl from where I swam, its low reverberation traveling through the water like thunder. He shifted into his human form and started stacking wood into a pile before forming a huge teepee with four long branches. With a thought, he had the pile engulfed in a blazing fire—a gift I had never known he possessed.

I sank beneath the surface and headed down to the bottom, thinking to make the man work to find me. It didn't take him long at all. My next thought was to out-submerge him. That didn't work either. He could hold his breath just as long as I could. We swam together, pointing out life and other things we swam across. Not wanting to be the first to rise, I fought the burn in my lungs. Finally, as if reading my body language, he grabbed my arm and pulled me with him to the surface.

My first breath was a deep one, seeing my poor lungs were nearly void of air. Ze, of course, was breathing as if he had done this all his life. When I could feel my lips again, I said, "Are you related to Superman or something?"

His answer was a deep kiss, covering my mouth as if he were taking his last breath. Hand wrapped through my hair, he pulled me closer, deepening the affection. It only made me want more. With hesitation, he pulled away. Now he was breathing hard. "I want you," he growled.

"I want you too, Zebastian. I'm sorry for what I said the other night. I didn't mean it."

"I know."

"Then why the silent treatment?"

"I needed time. You needed time."

Feeling my body shake with cold and my lips turning blue, I said, "Race you back?"

His brow arched. "You think you can win?"

I dove down and swam as if the devil were after me. Zebastian stayed just far enough ahead to make me try harder. When we reached the shore, he lifted me into his arms and carried me to the blazing fire.

"Damn, woman; you're freezing."

Despite my efforts to beat him to shore, my teeth were chattering, and my lips were now numb. "I may have stayed in a bit too long."

"You think?" Setting me down on a warm rock by the fire, he rubbed my skin with firm, vigorous strokes. "Where's your towel?"

"I didn't bring one," I chattered through my teeth.

He looked over at the clothes on the rock and then left to grab them. He set my pants and jacket by the fire to get warm. The shirt he used to dry me.

"What about you? Aren't you cold?"

"No." He continued to rub me down with the shirt until my skin started to feel warm. "Put your pants on and your jacket until this dries." He handed me the warmed clothes and then set my shirt over the rock to dry by the fire. "Wait here. I'll be back in a few minutes." Changing into his wolf, he dashed through the woods.

Heeding his suggestion, I donned the warm pants and jacket, and sat by the blazing fire. He returned shortly afterward with clothes in his mouth. I watched in dazed fascination as he changed back into his human form and donned the garments with practiced ease and grace.

"You really are a good-looking man, Zebastian."

He pulled his shirt down over his well-muscled stomach. "I'm glad you've finally noticed," he said with a teasing smile.

"Hmm, good-looking and humble."

Concern laced his stormy eyes; he looked toward the woods. "Are you warm enough to walk back to the cabin?"

"Yeah, what's wrong?"

"We're being watched." With a wave of his hand, he extinguished the fire. "Can you run?"

"Yes, of course."

"Listen. Stay close to me. If something happens, you run to the cabin and don't look back. Understand?"

"Ze, you're scaring me."

"Good." With that, he took my hand and we ran. It wasn't until we reached the cabin that he finally relaxed.

Teak met us in the den. "What's wrong?"

"Where's Khalen?"

"Pool room. Why?"

"Follow me?" He grabbed my hand and hauled me with him to the pool room as if letting me go would mean my death or something.

When my father saw us enter, his jaw grew tense. He set the pool cue down. "What's wrong?"

I felt him probing my thoughts, sensing my fear. When he looked at Zebastian, his eyes were glowing.

"Speak, Zebastian."

"The illusionist is here. I sensed him by the lake. He's not alone."

"Steed?" asked Teak.

Ze nodded.

"I'll strengthen my wards," said Father.

Ze released my hand. "I'm going back out there."

"I'll come with," said Teak.

Father nodded. "Keep your thoughts open."

I watched the two men leave the game room, striding as if fueled by adrenaline and a need to protect what was theirs.

~Zebastian~

BY THE TIME **T**EAK AND I reached the edge of the woods, Steed had vanished, along with his cohorts, leaving no trace of scent or presence.

"I can find them," said Teak, starting to remove his clothes.

"No, not today."

"They can't be far, Ze."

"They brought you down once. They'll do it again. I say we wait."

Teak's expression darkened, his thoughts turned inward and out of Ze's reach. "What are we waiting for?"

"They wanted us to know they were here."

"For what purpose? They have to know about Khalen's wards."

"Exactly. They expect Khalen to prepare for an attack that will never happen here."

"What do you propose?"

"Come with me," I said, heading back to the cabin.

I was able to fill Khalen in with a few simple thoughts. He was a clever man and not one to act with irrational abandon. It was something I had counted on.

"We are the most vulnerable while we are moving," said Khalen. "They expect us to move our clans."

"And if we don't?" asked Skye from the doorway. She was a sight with that long blonde hair flowing about her shoulders. Though she only stood about 5' 6", she stood taller than most females he knew and was worthy as a leader's mate—a position that took strength, courage, and intellect. She was the strength behind her male and the mother of future generations of leaders. Kaili had many of the same qualities.

"With enough force, they can break through my wards and possibly die in the process."

"They want me," I said. "I can lead them away from here."

Khalen started pacing before the fire in the hearth, sipping his brandy; the tap ... tap ... tap of his fingers against the glass filled the silence. "Aye, you could, but something tells me you are merely the tip of Bennet's iceberg. He does not think one dimensionally. He's much more clever than that."

"He's setting us up," said Aidan.

"Oh, aye; I'm sure he is."

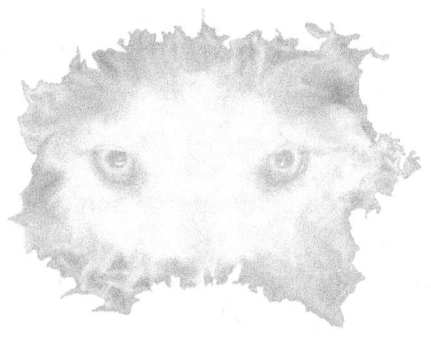

Chapter 20

~Kaili~

THIS WOULD BE ANOTHER SLEEPLESS night. Glancing at the clock, the blue numbers glowed 1:35. Zebastian's bed was empty. Since Seth and his mate had returned home, their room was available and he had moved into it. What I didn't understand was why.

Yes, I had been rather insistent about us not sharing this room, but that wouldn't be enough to sway him. I thought about what Teak had said to me in the foyer earlier about telling Ze the truth. I had been truthful, hadn't I? My gut sank as the memory of telling him that I faked our kiss to stop him replayed in my mind. That was a full-out lie and Ze knew it; he had to. He read my thoughts as easily as my father could, only Ze tapped my emotions as well.

I took another sip of tea, hoping the combination of chamomile and licorice would ease my mind and whirling thoughts enough for me to get some rest. The book I was reading lost my interest. What I needed was someone to talk to. Not just someone—Zebastian.

Easing out of bed, I wrapped myself in a robe and headed down the hall. If I remembered right, Ze's room was the last door on the left. It was open and light was flickering.

Ze sat up in bed, reading a book by candlelight. I knocked softly.

He looked up, but his emotions remained blank. "Kaili. Is everything all right?"

"May I come in?"

"Yes, of course." He put his book down on the end table and scooted over so I had room to sit. "Why are you still up?"

"Couldn't sleep."

"Worried about Steed?"

I thought about nodding to that, but in truth, I hadn't given the man or his threat much thought. Remembering what Teak said, I stopped my nod and said, "No, not Steed."

"What is it then?"

"I wanted to apologize to you."

His dark brows drew together. "For what?"

I knew his confusion was an act, but turnaround was fair play in the emotional arena, so I played along. "For lying to you the other day. I said I pretended to like our kiss to get you to stop. That was a lie. The truth is that you are the only man who has ever sparked my ..."

Despite my hint, he wouldn't complete the sentence. He, no doubt, wanted to hear the words from my lips, not just my mind.

"Desire," I finally spat out.

"And that frightens you?"

It shouldn't, I thought, but yes, it really did. "Odd, right?"

"No, not odd at all. When a man bonds with a female, it can be very threatening if the female does not feel the same toward the male."

"Bonded?"

"Yes, Kaili. I have bonded with you. I believe your father knows that."

I seriously doubted it. "If Father knew you had bonded with me, he would have you castrated."

The blank expression on Ze's face said otherwise. "Yet, he has offered me your first rights."

The words bounced around in my head like BBs in a jar. Had I heard him right? "Why would he do that?"

"You needn't worry," he said, his voice colder now, as if he had placed a brick wall between us. "I will honor your wishes, bonding or no."

I stood from the bed, feeling the need to run and escape. My wishes. What were they? Part of me wanted Ze; another part didn't know what I wanted. "We are too young," I blurted out loud.

"Both of us have come into our own, Kaili. We are old enough to unite."

"I don't even know what bonding feels like."

His pewter eyes seemed to take on a cloudy look in the candlelight. "When you feel it, you will know." There was sadness in his tone.

"When a male bonds, he can take no other until the female he has bonded with dies or unites with another. Correct?"

He nodded.

"Why would you do that, Ze?"

"It isn't something we control. It is a gift from the Father."

"Unless the bond isn't reciprocated; then it becomes

more of a curse, does it not?"

"The circumstances are rare, but yes, I could see it as a curse should the bond never be reciprocated."

So, if I never felt the same toward Ze, and we didn't unite, he would be repelled by every female out there until I died or mated with another male. How sick was that? I wasn't ready to unite. I wasn't ready to bond, yet if I didn't, Ze would be trapped in a hell I wouldn't wish upon anyone. What was wrong with me? Why didn't my heart function?

"Your heart functions just fine, Kaili," he said, his voice soft and loving. "You simply are not ready. I honor that. Take as much time as you need."

"You don't mean that," I said, my words coming out far more harshly than I intended. "What will you do when another man touches me?"

A low growl reverberated from deep in his chest—the reaction of a bonded male. It also served to make my point.

"Exactly," I said. "No matter where I am, you will feel it every time a man connects with me. No distance will separate us."

"I won't apologize for how I feel toward you, Kaili."

"I don't want you to."

"Then what do you want?"

Good question—one I had asked myself too many times to count. Deep down, I knew the base of my fears, my indecision. It was what my father and mother always worried over. In innocence, I would never be able to bond with any male, not completely. My body simply wouldn't know the difference. This was why it was important for young Spirians to connect with others; to have sex and experience what it felt like with various partners. In a moment, I knew exactly what I wanted from Ze.

"I want to give you my first rites—tonight." Before I lost my nerve, I removed my gown, allowing it to flutter to the floor. I was naked before him, as I was after our swim.

With his thoughts, he closed the door. "Very well. Come here, then." Lifting the covers, he patted the bed beside his naked body.

"I've never given first rights before, Kaili, and my experience was that of a slave, not a lover."

"Okay," I said, sliding in beside him. "We'll learn together, then."

The moment his body touched mine, my body reacted with a demand that caused my belly to ache. I felt empty inside, as if my core had been opened, leaving a huge void that needed to be filled. It wanted to be filled with him.

He cupped the side of my face with his huge palm, the warmth of it radiating down my neck and into my breasts. They, too, started to ache. My breathing quickened along with my pulse.

He smiled. "Your body's response pleases me."

I couldn't speak if I wanted to. Looking into his mesmerizing eyes, I felt paralyzed, trapped by his will. As his lips came down upon mine, I knew that I would never want another male's lips to take their place. Perhaps that was Ze's thoughts invading my own, but it didn't matter. That was how I felt.

His hand caressed my neck before easing downward. His touch made me crave for more. The ache in my body increased, but it wasn't a bad pain. It was a pain that I welcomed and now hungered for. As his hand drifted downward, my legs instinctively closed.

He moved them apart with his strong thighs. "Let me

do this," he whispered. He touched me then, sending a wave of heat through me that threatened to set me on fire. My breathing increased; my heart pounded as he continued to explore. Out of fear and panic, I tried to move away. His grip held me firm, keeping me in place.

"Shh," he cooed. "Relax, love. Don't fight me."

When his finger entered me, I froze.

"You're too tight. I need to prepare you."

"I'm scared."

He kissed me, somehow removing the fears from my thoughts. So many sensations flooded my body, driving me into an expansive bliss. I could feel his breath, his blood as it pumped in his veins.

When he rose above me, the sight of his erection raised a new level of panic. He was huge. "It won't fit," I warned him.

He cupped his hands on either side of my face. "Do you trust me?"

I nodded.

"I'll go slow. Your body will adapt."

He kissed me again, taking my mind to another place. Slowly, our bodies joined. Instead of the expected pain, all I felt was a hunger, a need to feel him deep inside. My hips rose to meet him, making him laugh a little.

"Easy, love. I need to go slow."

Forget slow. My body ached for more of him. It felt as if my muscles were drawing him inside. He gave me more, the size of him instantly felt. I gasped.

His kiss deepened, drowning out my renewed fear and anxieties. As my body arched to meet him, his groan vibrated against me, feeding my need. With a quick thrust, he entered me completely. The pain was sharp and quick. His mouth, still claiming mine, stifled my cry.

After giving me a moment, he started his movement again; this time he used longer, slower strokes. Together, we climaxed. His face strained; his veins stretched and pulsed with the beat of his heart. A strange, spicy scent surrounded me as he rolled us over onto our sides.

"You smell good," I said.

"It's my bonding scent. It's stronger in shifters."

It was all over me, like a perfume freshly sprayed. "I don't want to wash it off."

His smile warmed my heart. "You can't. It's not something that will leave you anytime soon."

I wondered how it would smell when mingled with my scented soaps and lotions. Somehow, lilac and clove did not seem like a good combination.

Again, he laughed. "My scent will rise above all others, love. It is not something that can be masked."

"I guess that's one way to keep other males from approaching me."

He growled. "Among others."

"Easy, Ze. I'm just saying. Honestly, I have no desire to see other males."

He held me tight, breathing in my scent. "This is a good thing."

I thought about Shaiya and the many males she had taken to bed. She did not share these emotional ties with any of them, I was sure. How could she? It couldn't be because Ze was my first. Shaiya's first had been just that: her first. She never saw him again, nor did she think or talk about him. Teak, on the other hand, was a different story. Shaiya seemed to like the male in more ways than just in bed.

Snuggled in tight with Ze still inside me, I dozed off, at peace for the first time in many nights.

Bang, bang, bang. "Ze!" The door opened and in stormed Teak, fully dressed and beaten to heck. Debris hung from his hair and clung to his bloody torso.

Ze, still holding tight, spun me around, placing me between him and the wall, away from Teak. Making sure I was completely covered, he turned toward his frantic friend.

"What is it, Teak? Where have you been?"

Teak flipped on the lights, giving a more detailed view of his injuries and condition. "I tracked Steed and his men. When I told Khalen, he and Gabrihen took off after them."

Ze sat up in bed. "I told you to leave it be!" The harshness in his tone made me shrink back. His hand reached around and held me to him.

Teak closed his eyes, his jaw corded with regret. "Khalen and Gabrihen are missing."

"Does anyone else know?"

Teak shook his head.

Ze looked back at me, his eyes focused inward as if he were thinking of a plan.

The quiet hum of Father's wards silenced. "Do you hear that?" I sat up, drawing the covers up with me. "Father's wards are down."

"Yeah," said Ze. He then looked to Teak. "Alert the others. Everyone meets in the great room."

Teak nodded, and then left.

A wave of panic ran through me. My father's presence could not be felt. It was as if someone had taken a piece of my soul, leaving an odd, cold void in its place. "I can't feel him, Ze."

"I know." He got out of bed and donned his jeans and shirt. "Get dressed. We have to leave."

I didn't want to leave him, but traveling in my robe was not an option, so I donned it and ran toward my bedroom. A cold presence awaited me.

Chapter 21

~Zebastian~

THE HAIR ON MY NECK stood alert with danger. I ran toward Kaili's room. A bear the size of a grizzly held her down, its claws inches from her throat. She was conscious, but barely. Her green eyes were glazed.

I transformed on the fly, my wolf's teeth tearing into the bear's back leg, rendering it useless. He spun to face me, either ignoring the pain of my attack or being numb to it. Telepathically, I told Kaili to leave.

She shook her head, sending me back an image that stated she wouldn't leave me alone with such a beast.

The bear came after me, claws flailing, teeth gnashing. His strength, as he tossed me against the wall, was supernatural. This was no ordinary bear shifter. He was a super shifter, which meant he wouldn't feel pain, and he wouldn't stop until he was dead. Again, he tossed me against the wall. The rage inside me took hold. The last thing I remembered was the bear going after Kaili.

I opened my eyes under the gazes of several concerned faces. Kaili knelt beside me, helping me sit. Death and destruction surrounded the place, rendering it into something unrecognizable.

"What happened?"

Aidan spoke first. "You were like a whirlwind, m'friend."

I looked around. Blood and flesh covered the walls and furniture.

"Your rage took over," said Teak. "Only I've never seen it in full force before. You had the speed of your panther and the power of your wolf combined."

Ian spoke next. "Ye have a bit of the reaper in ye as well. Two of the buggers dropped with merely your will for them t'do so."

I took a moment to gather my wits, to check Kaili from head to toe. "Are you all right?"

"I'm fine."

I brushed a speck of blood from her lip. "You're bleeding."

She scoffed. "It's a scratch, Ze."

I looked around but didn't see everyone. Struggling to my feet, I asked, "Where's Skye and Shaiya?"

Ian nodded to the master suite. "When all the commotion hit, Shaiya kept Skye in her room."

"Is she all right?"

Ian looked deflated. "She cannot feel Khalen."

Shaiya and Skye stepped out of the room, Skye looking stubborn and strong as always. "He's alive. I know he's alive."

Ian nodded. "Aye, lass, he's alive."

"Any word from Gabrihen?" I asked.

His friend, Connor, spoke up. "He's shielding himself."

"Or he's been captured with Khalen."

Skye reached over and touched my arm. "Why can't I feel Khalen?"

"They've taken him to an enclosure lined in lead. His powers are useless."

"Khalen doesn't need his powers to be dangerous," said Aidan.

"We need to find him," said Skye.

Aidan pulled her under his arm. "Easy, lass. We'll find them both, but we need to be smart about it."

Ian pulled out his cell phone. "We need to warn the clan."

"Right," Aidan agreed. "Call Arcadie and Case. I'll call Seth and Drew."

After they left the room, I looked to Teak. "Tell me what you know."

"Steed and five others were holed up in a house about five miles away. They looked vulnerable and unprepared for an attack. When Khalen and Gabrihen arrived, Steed's numbers increased tenfold. Steed disappeared during the fight and I lost track of him. The next thing I know, Khalen and Gabrihen are gone."

"An illusion, perhaps?"

Teak's face paled. "You warned me this would happen."

"Too late for regrets now, my friend. For now, we need to make sure the females are safe."

"I'm finding my mate," said Skye. "To hell with safe."

"It's too dangerous," I said. "If they get to you, they will have leverage over Khalen. He needs to know you're safe."

Aidan stepped into the room. "He's right, Skye. You and the girls must remain safe."

"I am his mate! If anyone can find him, it's me."

"Don't fight me on this, Skye—not on this."

The energy in the room increased, making my bones ache. "Skye, no one is stopping you."

Aidan stepped back, sensing the danger of touching her now. She was clearly not right in her head and in full protection mode. Most females didn't give off that kind of energy, but it was one that every male in the room knew better than to oppose.

"We just need to come up with a plan." I reached out to Aidan telepathically, letting him know we had to handle this situation in another manner. Forcing Skye to do anything but rescue her mate would be futile.

He nodded with acknowledgment.

"I'm coming too," said Kaili, setting off every protective instinct in me.

The low rumble coming from my chest did not go unnoticed. Every set of eyes turned toward me.

"Me too," Shaiya chimed in.

Ian raised his hands in defeat and started to pace. "Bloody hellish perfect!"

"Is there another clan we can go to?" I asked.

"Dean's clan is close," said Aidan. "We can get there within the hour."

Aidan pulled his cell phone out of his pocket. "I'll call him."

"I'll let Tisha know not to come for the next two weeks," said Skye.

"Good," I said. "We roll in twenty. Pack only what you need."

Teak and I both stiffened as we sensed other shifters mulling about the property. While the others left to pack their things, he and I ventured a look outside. As expected, more of those damn super shifters were gathering. We spotted at least ten of them so far.

I was hoping to have a quick shower, but that was not going to happen. "Stay inside," I told Teak.

"I can help."

"These are not regular shifters, my friend. Your eagle is hardly a match for their strength."

"I have something else in mind." Removing his clothes, he shifted into one of the biggest grizzly bears I had ever seen. He made Bender's bear look juvenile in comparison. He never used this animal before, but often spoke of him. Teak would still have a challenge with the super shifters, but he knew how to fight, and with a bear on his side, he would have an advantage.

"Nice."

I shifted into my wolf and we went to meet the intruders. I felt weak after my last battle, having reaped the lives of others. In our clan, reaping was considered a curse, which contributed to my father's decision to ban me from the clan, I was sure. It wasn't just about what happened to Carter. Father read my fears; being a reaper was one of them.

After observing Khalen and his gift, I decided it didn't have to be a curse if I could control it. The problem came with my rage and the blackouts that accompanied them. If I were unaware of what I was doing, innocent people could be hurt.

How any of this clan survived my last rage intrigued me, but there was no time to ponder that now. Five shifters encroached upon me. Reaping them was not an option; it would weaken me too much.

Teak took after three shifters, making quick work of the first—a tiger. The other two were easier opponents, a lynx and a fox. Teak would be fine.

From behind, a huge bear rose on its hind legs. I leapt forward, but a leopard bearing its teeth blocked my passage. The bear closed the distance, sinking his claws into my side, the pain like fire ripping through me. The leopard bit down on my throat. After that, everything went black.

~Kaili~

"**HELP HIM, MUM, PLEASE**," I cried, holding Ze tight in my arms. We had arrived at Dean's clan nearly an hour ago, but I had stayed in the car, too frightened to move Ze.

"He's healed, Kaili, but he's lost a lot of blood and his energy is nearly drained. He needs to rest now. Help me get him inside. Dean's mate, Katia, has a bed ready for him."

Ian scoffed. "The man's a true disaster when he's fighting. He must have dropped eight of them out there. For a moment, Teak, we thought you were a goner."

"I know better than to intervene," he said. "These rages of his are getting worse."

"Rages?" I asked.

"Yeah. When his adrenaline gets too pumped, he goes into this rage of sorts. He blacks out and remembers nothing. I've never seen him this fierce, though. He was like a man possessed out there. That gouge in his side and his open throat should have killed him. He fought, though, as if demons drove him on."

I brushed his damp face. "There are no demons in him."

Teak laid his hand on my shoulder. "I didn't mean it

that way."

Mum nodded to Aidan and Ian, gesturing them to take Ze from my arms. I released him with reluctance, allowing the brothers to pull him up and out of the car. I appreciated the care with which they handled him. On numb legs, I followed them into the guesthouse. The open layout allowed for many beds laid out along the three far walls, leaving space in the center. We would use the community privy and take our meals with the clan in the commons area.

This clan was much like ours on Harstine Island, only instead of cabins and yurts, Dean had constructed homes, giving it a village feel. There were even small shops where people could offer their goods and wares. No money was exchanged, of course, because the clan leader provided for everyone, as it was in all clans.

Once Ze was settled onto his cot, I covered him with blankets and took comfort in his slow and steady breath that made his chest rise and fall. "He's going to make it."

"Yes," said Mum, her hand resting gently over my shoulder. "He will. Just give him time."

Dean came in with a bag of blood and an IV kit. "We don't have much, but this should help."

Mum stepped forward, looked down at the blood bag as if she could see it, and frowned. "Wait. Let me make a call first."

Dean looked from her to his mate. "Okay."

Skye pressed the home button on her iPhone; the electronic voice chimed from the speaker. She said, "Call Seth."

The phone made a few chimes, and then said, "Calling Seth."

He must have answered because her eyes grew

brighter. "Seth. Something has happened. Zebastian's lost a lot of blood and we need to give him some."

Seth's voice rambled on the other end, his words too muffled for me to comprehend.

Mum nodded several times and bit her lower lip, her eyes dashing from the bag of blood to Ze. "Okay, Seth, thank you." Another pause followed by a glistening of unshed tears as I heard my father's name spoken. "No, not yet. We'll keep you informed." She hung up and slipped her phone into the pocket of her jeans.

"He cannot have that blood."

"Why?" asked Dean. "It is Spirian blood. It shouldn't affect a shifter."

"Seth believes that the blood will dilute his system too much and send him into anaphylactic shock."

Katia, a beautiful Russian woman with black hair and pale blue eyes, frowned in confusion. "I don't understand? He is shifter, yes?"

"Yes," said Mum, "but his blood has been modified by the same group of Shadows who have taken my mate. Zebastian's physiology has been modified."

"He's a super shifter," said Teak.

Ian and Aidan ushered the confused mated pair from the room, filling them in on the details telepathically. It was a much more elegant form of communication than words, but took great mental effort. Talking was much easier when in close proximity. Mental communication, however, could explain complex subjects in mere seconds and was used primarily for that purpose.

I wanted to crawl in beside Ze and feel his warmth against my skin, but the cot was far too small for the both of us. He alone took up the entire width of the thing.

"Let him rest, dear," said Mum. "You need something

to eat."

"I'm not hungry."

She paused for a moment, opened her mouth to speak, closed it again, lips firm and expressionless. *I understand,* she offered in thought before turning to leave.

Shaiya glanced over at me with a tender smile, and then wrapped her arm around Mum as they left the house.

Mum must be going through hell, I thought, not being able to feel Father. I believe all of us were going through the same thing to some degree. The clan leader was the foundation of the whole; when the leader was removed, the clan toppled like loose brick on shifting ground. Gabrihen was the next leader in line, but he was missing as well, making Aidan the temporary sachem. Father was alive, though; we all felt it, even though his presence was eerily absent. Gabrihen, too, was alive, but then so was Zhentu, and we hadn't been able to find him in years. My heart sank with the thought of not seeing my father and brothers again. Would my mother survive the ordeal? Would any of us?

Chapter 22

~ K h a l e n ~

I WOKE IN A CAGE IN which I barely fit. Curled into a ball, I lay on my side, feeling as if I had been hit by a meteor that had pounded me into the ground until my bones were nothing but dust. My head felt heavy, the voices of my clan silent. Skye—I couldn't feel her. I tried to bolt up, but connected with an iron bar that split the top of my scalp. We were in a truck that just plowed over what felt like a pothole the size of a car.

"Easy, mate."

I turned to see a lanky man with dark hair and the eyes of an illusionist. "My family," I groaned.

"Are no longer your concern."

I knew they weren't dead. If they were, I'd feel it. "Who are you? Where are you taking me?"

He stared out the barred window that spanned the length of the truck bed. Given the scent that wafted through, we were passing through snow territory ... heading northeast.

Venturing a guess, I asked, "You work for Bennet?"

More silence. The man's jaw worked as if the name had spurred emotions that mimicked rage. I tried tapping his thoughts, but it was as if my gifts had been stripped, which explained why I couldn't reach out to my clan and mate.

"I can help you," I said.

He scoffed, bending a half smile that gave his features a sinister edge. "You can't even help yourself, mate."

"Get me out of here and I'll see that you're protected."

"And what of my mate and daughters? Can you help them as well?" The anger in his eyes was sharp as shattered glass.

"Is that what this is about? Bennet holds your family in exchange for mine?"

"Now you have the gist of it. Though, I fear that handing Bennet your family won't be enough to save them."

"Then you have nothing to lose by letting me go."

His laser-etched eyes turned to me, narrowed and dull like a man who had lost his will. "I don't give a damn about you and your family."

My neck sported a metal collar that felt like acid against my skin. Pulling on it only increased the pain.

"The collar is made of lead, mate. It is how he will control you. So long as it is activated, you will be without your gifts."

"Where are you taking me?"

Silence. His eyes glazed over as the truck continued to roll on. He remained that way for the duration, despite my attempts to sway him. When the truck finally pulled to a stop, I scented saltwater, algae, and—.

Clang, scrape, bang, followed by a squeak as the door swung open. The brightness of the day indicated it was just past noon, which meant we had been on the road for at least six hours. The man riding beside me climbed out.

"Should we keep him caged?" asked a rather large man with very sparse hair and a face that resembled a billiard ball.

"No need. His collar is activated. Any attempt of attack or escape will shock him into unconsciousness."

With caution, the large man reached in and unlocked the cage. "Out with you, then. Come on."

Peeling my body free of the confines of the cage, I bit back the pain that shot through my body as it straightened. The large man grabbed my arm and flung me onto the ground, before hauling me back to my feet.

"I don't want no trouble from you. Understand?"

He was the only man, besides the one who had ridden with me in the truck. Spinning around, I struck the larger man in the throat, felling him to the ground. My collar buzzed, sending a shock that made lightning seem like a hand slap. I dropped to my knees, my body tingling with the effect of several volts shooting through my body.

The slim man laughed. "Perhaps you didn't hear me mention the collar and the insurance it provides?"

He nodded to someone, but I couldn't see who past the truck. Two more men came, hauling my limp body down to a dock where a boat was tied.

"Get him onboard and then wait for me."

The two men nodded. One of them sported a fedora while the other allowed his overgrown hair to play folly with the wind. Both were dressed in Carhartt jeans and jackets.

The dark-haired man, who accompanied me in the truck, said something to the truck driver I had slammed to the ground, and then ran toward us.

"Is he all right?" asked the man in the cap.

"He'll live," said dark hair, climbing onto the boat. "Let's go."

My first thought was to throw myself out of the boat, but given the low water temperature and that I still could not move my limbs, I decided against it. As if reading my mind, dark hair clamped his hand around my upper arm.

An hour later, we arrived on a rock with jutting cliffs. It looked dead to me, and perhaps to most people who happened by the island en route to better destinations. The two thugs wearing Carhartt hauled me by my arms to an area that simply looked like granite. Dark hair made a quick phone call, and the stone facade swung open.

Bennet was an elementist with earth-bending properties. He, no doubt, had purchased the small island and built a fortress within the towering cliff. With his gifts, he could make the rock resemble anything he wanted with a mere thought, making it a nightmare to those who might be trapped inside. It took great skill to do so, but then Bennet was a man of great promise, which explained his power over the entire eastern coast. As a Shadow, he was my equal.

"Take him below," ordered dark-hair.

My feet dragged behind me in the candelabra-lit corridor as the two men hauled me to a room of empty cages. Without ceremony, they tossed me inside a cell and slammed the door shut. The cold dampness indicated we were below sea level. The men filed out, leaving me alone.

~ Bennet ~

WHEN STEED KNOCKED ON THE door, I opened it with my will and gestured him inside. "Do you have something for me?" I asked.

"I do, m'lord."

His new title for me was pleasing. It was a new addition since my last instructions in respect were issued; nice to know he had learned his lesson. "Well, what is it?"

He swallowed hard a few times, keeping a healthy distance between us ... smart man. What he lacked in brawn, he made up for in brains, which was what was needed to capture the North American leader. Khalen was smart and powerful, making him a challenging and delightful opponent. It would be a treat seeing him squirm under my authority.

"Khalen awaits you downstairs, m'lord."

The sound of the leader's name made my heart do the pitter patter with a shot of adrenaline for emphasis. At the risk of sounding overly pleased or eager, I added a pause before asking, "Is he ... restrained?"

"Yes, he's wearing a collar and is in the cell room."

"And the others?"

Steed shifted like a child who had just soiled his pants. "Their capture is in process, m'lord."

"In process? I find that hard to believe when you stand here before me."

"I wanted to escort Khalen to you personally, m'lord; to ensure he arrived without mishap."

"Who is leading the others' capture?"

"Granger. I sent him with a band of super shifters."

"Granger," I growled, knowing the man to be an idiot if not a bungling fool. "The man is muscle without a brain, all brawn with no thought of how to wield it wisely."

"I gave him precise orders, m'lord."

I pointed toward the door. "Go back and make sure he followed them. If not, I'll take it out on your hide."

The man actually bowed ... good.

"Yes, m'lord."

"And, Steed."

He froze, hand on the handle of the door. "Yes, m'lord." He turned around slowly, as if suddenly remembering how rude it was to address the leader without turning about.

"I expect you back here shortly, with the others?"

He swallowed hard and closed his eyes. "Yes, m'lord."

"Good."

I watched him leave, listening to his footsteps as he clambered down the hall. Had he captured Khalen? It was a possibility beyond my expectations. The chance of him catching a rainbow would be more plausible. Setting the Aussie up with an impossible task, however, was the only way to keep him engaged. Otherwise, his contract would end too quickly, and that would be a waste; it truly would.

I poured myself a brandy and started for the door, hesitated, and then went back to pour a glass for Khalen—a gesture I was sure he'd appreciate.

Seeing it was several flights down, I took my time descending the stairs, marveling at the structure of the place. It was my wizard's best work and I found that stone made an excellent insulator. This granite castle was almost as pleasing as my mansion in upstate New York. I didn't frequent this castle enough. I had a feeling that would change, however, once I had Khalen and his family contained. The thought of his daughters and mate in my possession offered great pleasure.

I rounded the corner and willed the lights on. It was

cold down here—too cold. Knowing the place was heated from below, this lower level should have been warmer.

As I entered the cell room, two of my technicians were busy working in the lab. One look from me prompted them to take leave. Khalen was my only captive. The others had been released to the world to do my bidding. With an army of super shifters, I would become unstoppable.

Khalen sat meditating in the darkest corner of his cell, eyes closed, body still as calm water. I kicked the cell door, causing it to rattle.

"Wakie, wakie."

His golden eyes opened slowly, a slight glow shimmering behind their irises—interesting. His collar should have prevented that glow, provided it was still functional. If it weren't, Khalen would come after me with a vengeance I would be hard pressed to stop.

"How are you feeling?" I asked, trying to rouse him. "Would you like a drink?" Carefully, I lowered the glass to the floor and slid it between the bars, all the while keeping my eye on the leader.

Still, he said nothing. Fortunately, the glow behind his eyes dimmed. That was promising.

"Your family will be joining you soon."

A low growl sounded from his chest ... another good sign.

"I look forward to getting to—know your mate and two lovely daughters."

He unfolded his legs, stood from his cot, and strode toward the bars, his eyes never leaving mine.

"You touch my family, Bennet, and I will personally see your soul enter hell."

Amused by his boldness, I laughed. "And how, pray tell, do you intend to do that, dear boy? In case you haven't noticed, your powers have been stripped, and any attempt to escape or attack will render you useless. By the way, that collar looks spectacular on you."

He returned to the cot, eyed the drink, then walked back over to get it.

"I knew you could be reasonable," I said. "Your son fares well, by the way."

He looked over at me through narrowed slits. "Which one?"

"Zhentu, your youngest. He has your spirit, you know—completely uncontrollable."

"That should serve as a warning to you," he said, fingering his collar.

"Yes, well, in time, he will break; they always do."

"As will you."

"I'm afraid you underestimate me. You have been a leader for what? A mere twenty-plus years? I have been one for a century. My power exceeds yours tenfold."

"If power is all you have, Bennet, you will lose this battle, I assure you."

I took a sip of my brandy and started pacing, trying to keep the cold from entering my bones. "Don't count on your clan to help you, Khalen. They are under attack as we speak, including the clan in Uig. Especially the one in Uig," I added with a growl.

His lack of reaction disturbed me. Was the man numb? Had they drugged him? He just sat there, holding his drink, staring straight ahead.

"Did you hear what I said, Khalen? Your clans are destroyed ... gone. Everyone will die."

"Is that what this is about, Bennet? The fact that Raeiza joined with my nephew instead of with you?"

"That female was mine. I paid for her."

"So you took Zhentu as retribution?"

"I took Zhentu for his blood. With it, I was able to create an army that cannot be defeated."

"Save by one."

That got my attention. So, he knew about my super shifter, the one who got away? Funny how Steed failed to mention that tidbit of information. "What do you know about him?"

"You won't turn him. He'll never obey."

I tried reading his thoughts, but the collar he wore blocked me. "What is his name?"

"You will find out soon enough."

Chapter 23

~Gabrihen~

THE GAPING INJURY IN MY side continued to bleed and I knew I didn't have much time before I passed out, but I wasn't going to leave my father. They had taken him. I needed to find out where before alerting the others. Tearing another section from my disheveled shirt, I wadded the scrap up and packed it into my wound. It wouldn't stop the bleeding, but it would help to slow it down.

Transporting myself hadn't helped matters either, but I had no other choice. I had to stay with the truck that held my father and follow him to his destination. Once they had carried him to the island, I had lost my connection to him. The collar they had placed around his neck blocked our thoughts.

Now that I knew where they held him, it was time to transport myself back to the cabin. When I arrived, the horror that greeted me robbed my knees of strength. I sank to the ground, blackened and singed with burn marks. The cabin was torched to the ground. I felt the clan; they were alive. Mentally, I reached out to Mum.

Mother?

She answered straightaway, having stayed in tune for Father and me. *Gabrihen, where are you?*

The cabin ... too weak to transport.

Wait there. I'll send someone for you.

I hadn't the strength to move. If the attackers came back, I wouldn't be able to defend myself against them. Closing my eyes, I prayed for more time.

W ARMTH SURROUNDED MY BODY as I woke to the sound of a crackling fire and the scent of bitter tea.

"Mum," Kaili's voice muttered. "He's awake."

The blurred image of my mother dominated my field of vision as she leaned over me. The feel of her hands sent waves of heat through my body, energizing my spirit. My vision started to clear.

"Gabrihen," she whispered, her voice like a distant angel. "Come on, son; wake up."

"Mum," I said, my voice sounding like gravel. I tried sitting up, fighting a wave of dizziness.

She helped stabilize me, as Kaili stuffed pillows behind my back.

"Father is in trouble," I said.

My mother's eyes looked hopeful. "You know where he is?"

I nodded, immediately regretting that decision. My head pounded with every beat of my heart. "He's being held on an island; East Coast. The rock is impenetrable."

Aidan came to my side. "Where lad?"

I sent him an image of what I had seen. "He wears a collar. I saw it shock him."

Mum stumbled backward, landing hard on the couch beside me.

"Easy, lass," said Aidan. "We'll find him."

"Who has him?" asked Mum.

"I don't know. I've never seen him before." I sent them the man's image.

Tetris, my old mentor, stepped forward, warming his hands by the fire. Mum must have called him to find me. He was a powerful wizard who could transport multiple people with minimal effort. "One of Bennet's blokes, perhaps?"

I looked around the strange house, recognizing nothing but my immediate family. "Where are we?"

"Dean's clan," said Aidan. "We're safe here."

"Where's Zebastian and Teak?"

"They travel north, trying to gain enforcements," said Aidan.

Mum handed me the bitter cup of tea. "Drink this. It will help build your blood."

Ian stepped into the room, slipping his iPhone into his pocket. "Harstine Island's been hit, as well as Uig."

Aidan's jaw tightened. "Any casualties?"

"Drew moved the lot in time and Seth has everyone underground. No casualties."

"Any word from Arcadie and Case?"

"They're on their way. Should land at the airport in three more hours."

I drank the tea, cringing at the poignant flavor. "If Bennet is involved, we will be seriously outnumbered."

"Especially if those cursed super shifters stand guard," said Ian. "They are not affected by our illusions and they're as strong as twelve men. If Zebastian were not on our side, we would be dead for sure."

"Is Khalen hurt?" the soft voice of my mother asked.

"No, he's fine," I assured her. "Mad as hell, but whole. He drained himself by taking out several shifters, which is why they were able to swarm him so quickly. They shot him with something. I was going to attack, but I figured I would be more useful if I could follow them, instead."

"Smart man," said Aidan. "That was the right decision, lad."

"Yes," Mum agreed. "Thanks to you, we will be able to find him."

Tetris spoke next. "With that wound you were sportin', I'm impressed with what you were able to do, lad. Your father will be proud, for sure. I know I am."

I felt my face warm with the compliment. Praise was not something Tetris touted often. Whether or not my father was proud was yet to be proven. I hadn't seen him that enraged for a very long time.

I looked over at Kaili, who, unlike her twin, looked somber and troubled. I reached over and touched her hand. "Hey, are you okay?"

She nodded and then frowned. "Ze has his thoughts closed to me. I can't read him."

"I'm sure he's fine."

"He's either not in his shifter form, or he's keeping me out for a reason."

Mum came over and offered her a hug. Shaiya, too, joined in. It was the female version of bonding, I supposed. Personally, I preferred a good fight and a cold beer over all that touchy-feely crap.

"So, what's the plan?" I asked Aidan.

"We storm the castle and get our leader back."

"God help us," said Tetris.

~Zebastian~

MONITORING KAILI'S THOUGHTS, **I** learned where Khalen was taken. I also learned that she and her mother and sister were planning to be part of his rescue. How Ian and Aidan were going to allow that, I would never know. The females were strong, yes, but in battle, they would be turpentine on a blazing fire. I would address this concern with Kaili after Teak and I settled down for the night.

I sensed Kaili's concern for me as she tried multiple times to tap my thoughts. I kept her out, knowing that other shifters could listen in. Once they discovered my feelings for her, she would be used as a weapon against me. God only knew how that would pan out. I didn't want to find out.

Teak flew high above me as we traveled north. We would have to stop soon for food and time to rest. Shifters could travel for miles between meals and sleep, but there were still several miles to go, and allowing ourselves to grow weak in the journey would only give our enemies an unnecessary advantage. Ian had offered us his Jeep, but traveling by land would cut out several miles, and was far less conspicuous.

Are you up for some elk? Teak asked in thought, showing me a nearby herd. I headed east, keeping downwind. I scented other predators in the area. No doubt, they could sense me as well, making this possible hunt a bit more treacherous. Most territorial battles ended in death.

Releasing the bag I carried, I spotted a yearling as a possible target. In a flash, a mountain lion sprinted after the herd. I moved in as well. Following the lioness, I found the target of her interest: a cow with a young calf. As the mountain lion took the cow down, I went after the calf, seeing he wouldn't survive without his dam anyway. It was a perfect kill; one without waste. The cow would feed the mountain lion while the calf provided for Teak and me. What we didn't finish, the scavengers would relish; such was the way of nature. Nothing went to waste.

The calf was big, weighing close to 300 pounds. Dragging him to our campsite was unrealistic, so I bit off a hind quarter and left the rest.

Teak circled above, indicating he had found a place to camp for the night. Using the mental image he'd sent me, I went back for my bag and carried it and the hind quarter north up the mountain.

By the time I got there, Teak had gotten dressed and had a fire burning. My body was weary from travel and ready to rest. We still had several miles to cover, but if we got an early start, we could make it to the northern clans by nightfall tomorrow.

The sound of a nearby stream sounded too inviting to resist, so I left to bathe myself. I returned to the scent of cooking meat that Teak had stripped and skewered over the fire. I preferred to have my meat slow roasted, but we were both too tired to wait that long. The meat would cook in minutes this way, though it would not be nearly as flavorful.

I tossed my empty bag aside and sank beside him by the fire.

Teak looked over at me and smiled. "Long day, yeah?"

"Yeah," I sighed.

"Any word from the clan?"

I fished my cell phone out from my pocket and glanced at the screen. "Khalen's father and uncle have arrived. Gabrihen returned. He knows where they have taken Khalen."

"All good news."

I frowned, realizing there was nothing from Kaili.

"Call her," said Teak. "She's probably worried."

"And what of your female? Does she not worry as well?"

"Shaiya is hardly my female. We enjoy each other's company, yes, but she is not mine."

"Does she know that?"

He twisted a twig and tossed it into the flames. "Oh yes, she's made it crystal clear. The man who captures her heart will have to make the stars align in the sky and change the moon's color at her whim."

"So, what are you waiting for?" I asked in jest.

"Call your female."

I stood and walked to where the signal was stronger, preparing myself for a tongue lashing that would make Khalen's reprimands feel like silk to the skin. The phone rang once, twice.

"Ze?"

"Hey, love."

"Are you all right?"

My heart swelled, hearing that was her first question. "Yes, we are fine. We should arrive in the northern territories by tomorrow's eve."

"Your thoughts have been closed to me."

I closed my eyes, knowing that any explanation I offered would not be the right one. My mother had taught me that. No wrath equals the fury of a worried female. "There are Shadows about. I do not want them to learn my feelings for you. It's too dangerous."

"Your scent is all over me, Ze. Do you think there is a male who can approach me without knowing your claim?"

The thought of my scent on her pleased me as I remembered our night together; how she felt in my arms, beneath me and around my erection, which now stood proud with the thought and longed to repeat the experience. "I want to keep you safe."

"Do not shut me out, Ze. Ever."

"I do it for your own good."

Silence—never a good sign.

"Kaili, please."

"I can sense your thoughts without them knowing, Ze. Please don't shut me out."

I now knew Khalen's frustration with Skye and how she manipulated her words to suit her purpose. Her daughter had the same gift—lucky me. "Very well."

"Thank you."

"If you are captured due to my carelessness, know that your father will have my balls in his fists."

"I am not without my defenses, Ze."

"You are an unclaimed female. If captured, you will not be able to defend yourself against Shadow males."

"Your scent will keep them at bay."

Or draw them closer, I feared. "Stay with the clan, Kaili, please. Do not wander off on your own."

"You have my word."

"Thank you. Get some rest now. I'll call tomorrow."

"Good night, Ze. Stay safe."

The silence of the phone left my heart heavy. I didn't like the distance that spanned between us, and I found myself envious of Gabrihen's gift of transporting through space—lucky bastard.

When I returned to the fire, Teak had already started eating off one of the skewers. As I sat, he handed another one to me.

"How did it go?"

"Good," I said, ripping a chunk of meat from the skewer.

"Yet, your heart is heavy."

"I fear I have placed her in danger."

"We are all in danger at this point, my friend. Bennet has made it so."

"But he's after me."

"Khalen believes otherwise."

That got my attention. "Tell me what you know."

"Rae, Seth's mate, was destined to join with Bennet. When that didn't happen, and Seth claimed her first, Bennet retaliated by taking Khalen's son, Zhentu."

"So my involvement is a mere convenience for Bennet."

"Perhaps. Either way, we are all in danger unless we gain help from your father's tribes."

"I pray he'll listen to me."

Teak's brows arched upward as if doubting that was the worst of my problems. "I pray he doesn't kill you."

Chapter 24

-Zebastian-

IT **WAS DARK BY THE** time we reached our home clan. I felt my father's men surround us as Teak and I approached. Father, himself, met us at the territories' edge, probably having felt our presence many miles away. It was his gift, among many. Despite the fact that he had banned me, I still respected the man like no other. My heart ripped at the thought of being his bane.

"Father," I said, bowing my head in respect.

"Do not call me so!" he roared, causing the trees to tremble. His eyes glowed green against the moonlight.

"Apologies, sire."

"I see Khalen did not endeavor to kill you."

The hair on the back of my neck stood guard as wolves, panthers, and bears surrounded us. Their scent reeked of adrenaline as if they were amped for a fight.

Teak felt them, too, his bear itching to get out. I silently warned him to calm the beast, lest we find ourselves in an outnumbered fight.

"Ask your men to back off. We are not here for trouble."

"You enter my territory unannounced. I'd say you found trouble."

A black wolf approached my left flank, his teeth bared, a growl rumbling from deep in his chest. I recognized him as Galock, an aggressive male nearly twice my age. We never did get along due to my relations with Teak, whom Galock viewed as below my status. He always was opinionated. Father's ban of me must have elevated Galock's status within the tribe.

When Teak's protective instinct kicked in, my father brought him to his knees.

"You will stay out of this," he warned.

"Tiban," Teak struggled to say, "please, listen to him. We come here asking for help." As my father's energy increased, Teak struggled to stay upright on his knees.

Galock closed in. If I engaged him as my wolf, my rage would kick in, and God knew what would happen or whom I would choose to attack. Galock was leaving me little choice, however.

I looked over at Teak, who mouthed, "Don't," warning me of what I already knew. Father was proving a point, I was sure. I was a monster to destroy. Unfortunately, he had no idea what kind of monster he was about to unleash.

Somehow, I had to maintain control, or lose father's respect forever. I thought about what Khalen had once told me, when we discussed his gift of reaping. He said we were responsible for our own actions, always, regardless of the situation. When Khalen reaped, he maintained control. I would have to learn to do the same, lest my rage define my fate.

Galock's attack was quick and precise. He bit into my hip, provoking my anger. If I didn't control my rage before I shifted, I would not be able to do so as my wolf.

Taking a few deep breaths and ignoring the burning pain, I centered my thoughts, filling them with images of Kaili lying naked beneath me, her green eyes misty with pleasure, her mouth soft and slightly swollen from my kisses.

Before Galock's teeth connected with my leg, I sprung away, changing into my wolf on the fly. It was a difficult feat to perform, and I felt both my father and Galock's surprise toward my skill.

Galock and I circled one another, our growls reverberating off the trees, sounding vaguely of thunder. Father stood back while Teak watched on with glistening eyes, racked with pain. The result of this fight would determine both our fates.

Acting the submissive, I allowed Galock to make the first move. He was a skilled fighter and fierce with claws and teeth. The power of him had improved since our last tangle, as had his speed. He caught me off-guard, knocking me to the ground. His teeth sank into my scruff. I rolled and shook him off. Two more attacks and I would finish the fight. It wouldn't take long. Galock, despite his skill, was no match for a super shifter.

Before it got that far, Father sent two more of his shifters upon me: a panther and another wolf. I did not recognize either of their scents. Had Father recruited from other clans?

Now I had three shifters to battle. If I didn't end things quickly, I would soon be fending off the entire pack of twelve. This, of course, did not concern me as much as keeping my rage at bay.

I sent a silent plea to Kaili, asking her to mind my rage and keep my thoughts calm. I respected her for not asking a million questions right now. She instinctively knew to stay silent unless needed.

The two wolves attacked. I had to incapacitate Galock and remove him from the equation. The panther joined in, giving Galock an opportunity to sink his teeth into my side, drawing blood. I felt my rib crack under the pressure and it stole my breath. I felt my rage on the edge.

Focus, Kaili's sweet voice echoed in my head. *Go for their weaknesses.*

Spinning around, I caught the panther by its slender neck and flung it away. It slammed against a tree, crumpling to the earth like a boneless heap. Galock gripped my foreleg. My teeth removed his ear as I slammed him to the ground. Before the other wolf could find purchase, I sidestepped, allowing his attack to follow through to Galock. The wolf howled as Galock tore into his throat.

The remaining pack began to close in, but Father's hand stopped them. Now, it was just Galock and I facing off, both bloodied and fueled by pain. My rage hovered like a fog rolling in, threatening to blind my rationale.

You can do this, I heard in my head. *Focus on my voice.*

Father gave Galock a hand signal I did not recognize and the wolf came in for the kill. Before his teeth could tear into my jugular, I spun away and pinned the black beast with my teeth over his throat, holding him there until his body relaxed, indicating defeat.

He rose, shifted into his human form, and then bowed to my father. I shifted as well, grabbing the clothes that were tossed to me. Donning them, I looked to my father, gauging the light in his eyes to be something I hadn't seen for quite some time: pride.

He released Teak from the painful energetic bind before speaking. "You fought well."

I wasn't sure whether he addressed me or Galock.

When Father's eyes locked onto mine, it took everything I had not to look away as I had been taught to do so many years past. Doing so showed submission, something I truly did not feel.

When father raised his chin a notch, I stood my ground, continuing to meet his stare.

"Leave us," he told his horde.

Galock looked at me, his jaw tight and corded. When I met his stare, he immediately looked away and followed the others into the woods.

Teak stumbled over to a fallen log and sat, still green from the effects of the bind.

Again, I met Father's eyes. "I came to ask for your help on Khalen's behalf."

His brows rose slightly. "You serve him now?"

I never liked that term; it was one reserved for pets and slaves, neither of which defined me. "I support his clan in this matter."

"Defiant to the end, I see."

"Bennet Graves is trying to take over the northern territories. He has captured Khalen and plans to destroy his family. We need the support of your clan in this matter."

"Bennet has no claim here. His forces are not enough to take this territory."

"He has built an army of super shifters, those who cannot be killed so easily."

He scoffed. "Monsters, like yourself."

"Ze is not a monster," said Teak.

Father's energy rose. I stood between him and my friend.

"This is not about me. This is about Khalen and his need for help. Are you willing?"

"Yes, of course."

I sent him images of the location Aidan had shared with me. "We believe he is held here. To destroy Bennet, we must eliminate him and his associations."

"We move tomorrow," he said.

"Thank you."

"As you said, this has nothing to do with you. Our regional leader needs help. We are his loyal guard, always."

I nodded. "Very well."

"Does he know what you are?" he asked as I turned to leave.

I stilled, and then turn to face him. "Khalen sees me for what I am."

"Yet he lets you live and serve his clan?"

Teak stood, looking as if he intended to take on the leader—a feat Teak would not survive. I gripped his arm and shook my head no.

"He insults you," Teak growled.

"Let us take our leave," I told him. "He will think what he may. It doesn't matter."

Teak shook my hand free. Giving the leader one last look, he followed me into the woods, opposite the direction Father's guards had taken.

"Truth will reveal itself in time," my father called out as Teak and I slipped through the trees.

"Damn his heart," Teak growled.

"Easy, Teak. He is still my father, no matter his beliefs about me."

"Forgive me, my friend. The man tries my patience and toys with my loyalty."

I smiled at him, knowing exactly where his loyalties lay. Teak had been the only solid thing in my life. No matter what, he stood by my side, much like Aidan and

Ian stood by Khalen's. "Even the mouse knows to still himself until his predator grows bored."

"Speaking of stilling one's self, you were quite impressive during that fight. I half-expected you to check out several times."

"You can thank my angel for that."

"Kaili?"

I nodded.

"She is good for you, Ze."

"That she is," I agreed.

My cell phone vibrated. I pulled it from my pocket and saw it was the young wizard.

"Gabrihen."

"Dean's clan was attacked."

Chapter 25

-Kaili-

ONE MINUTE, SHAIYA AND I were standing with our mum; the next, we were sitting in a cage in the back of a dark truck, our hands tied behind our backs. We weren't moving and Mum wasn't with us. A point on the side of my neck felt raw and tender, as if it had been struck by something. My head still foggy, I wondered whether I was only imagining Ze's voice in my head.

"Where are we?" Shaiya groaned.

"I don't know."

Kaili, Ze's voice reached out to my mind in the language of his wolf.

I'm here. Are you all right?

Fine. Where are you?

Captured. I sent him images of my cage and the inside of the truck. I felt him scan my senses for scent and sight.

I'll find you.

The door to the truck slammed open. Light pierced my eyes as I opened my mind to Ze.

I'm scared, I told him.

I felt the warmth of his thoughts embrace me, giving me strength.

Rough hands reached into my cage and hauled me out, flinging my body to the hard ground, knocking the wind from my lungs. More strong hands gripped me while a collar was secured to my neck. The world felt eerily silent and my soul felt drained.

Shaiya received the same treatment.

I tried reaching out to Ze but the connection was severed. The warmth of him was stripped away through the coldness of the collar.

Steed stepped around the truck. "Well, well, what do we have here?"

Still foggy from whatever they'd shot in me, I struggled to focus on his willowy frame. Funny, before Ze, Steed seemed like a solid male in both stature and looks. Now, he resembled a weasel on spindly legs. His face was drawn and he looked to have aged a century. Darkness had that effect on a soul.

He took out his phone and dialed a number. When the other party answered, Steed turned away and started walking back to the front of the truck. Two men marched Shaiya and me toward a dock. They didn't talk much, but they smelled like rotten eggs.

"Where are they taking us?" asked Shaiya.

"Maybe to where they have Father?" Wishful thinking, anything to keep fear from my thoughts.

Shaiya remained quiet and that, in itself, worried me. Shaiya was never quiet even in stressful situations. The drug must be having a lasting effect.

Steed joined us on the dock. "The boat is on its way. You are instructed to take the females to the lower cell room where Bennet will come to collect them."

The men nodded and Steed offered one last look to Shaiya and me before heading back to the van.

We had some time before the boat would arrive. I wasn't sure how much time, but seeing there was no boat in sight, I assumed we had at least five to ten minutes. When I glanced over at Shaiya, she seemed to be on board with whatever I had in mind. There were only four men. If we could disable two of them right away, we might stand a chance with the other two—or so we thought.

The moment we tried to stomp our feet down onto our captor's instep, a shock equal to a lightning strike coursed through our bodies, rendering them slack and useless. It took everything I had just to regain my breath. This explained why Father was still detained—if he wore a collar such as this, he would be just as helpless.

So, there my sister and I lay on the hard deck, unable to move, and shivering with cold. Thirty minutes must have passed before the men sighted the boat.

~Khalen~

THE DOOR CLANKED OPEN. ANOTHER visit from Bennet perhaps? When I saw my two daughters being dragged over the floor, my instincts took over, followed by a shock that dropped me to my knees.

Kaili and Shaiya were tossed into a cell with little care, their bodies limp.

"No!" I yelled.

Two men secured my daughters' cell, and then left without sparing me a glance or a word. They were minions, trained to say nothing, feel nothing, and do only what they were told. Talking to them would be a waste of air.

"Kaili, Shaiya," I called to them.

"Father," they replied.

"Did they hurt you?"

Kaili glanced over at him through the darkness, her green eyes looking gray and drawn. "No, but this collar packs quite a charge."

"Yes, I haven't found my way around it yet."

"I can't move."

"It takes time to wear off. Your mum, is she—" he couldn't finish the sentence, not wanting to believe she had been taken or hurt. If she had died, he would have felt it, so he knew she was still alive—somewhere.

"I don't know."

"I'm cold," said Shaiya. "So very cold."

I closed my eyes, wanting to rush to their side and protect them, keep them warm. "I know, sweetheart. Practice your breathing. Do you remember what I taught you?"

"I remember," she said.

"Good. Do it now; it will bring warmth to your body."

I heard both of them practice the nine-breath technique. The exercise would not only raise their core temperatures, but it would serve to calm their minds as well.

Two hours later, they were standing and pacing before the bars that separated us. I was able to control the collar somewhat, but my energy drained too quickly to have lasting effects.

"What do they want with us?" asked Kaili.

"I'm not sure."

The door opened and in stepped Bennet with two more thugs. "Aw, the happy family reunites. How sweet."

There was no use in replying. I needed to keep my

anger in check, conserve my energy for a more productive course.

The thugs opened my daughters' cell, pulling them out one at a time.

"Oh my," said Bennet, running his hand down the side of Kaili's face. "How lovely." He repeated the action on Shaiya. "I look forward to claiming them."

The growl in my throat vibrated against the stone walls. "Touch them, Bennet, and I will see your soul to hell."

"That would be a neat trick considering the position you're in. Weak as a kitten, I believe is the phrase."

When Bennet touched Kaili's lips, she bit down hard, drawing blood. Impressively, she did not relinquish her hold even as the collar zapped her down.

Bennet screamed like a child as he tried to break free, dislocating his finger in the process. With a hard hand, he came down on Kaili, splitting her lip. Not even a whimper escaped her lips. She just smiled as if asking him to try it again. When Bennet pulled back his boot for a kick, Shaiya planted one of her own, right in his face. The sound of his breaking nose was sharp against the stone walls.

Again, he cried and wailed, kicking Shaiya's fallen body with the point of his boot. The blow took her wind and caused her to heave, but she didn't cry out. My girls were tough, just like their mother.

"Take them to my chamber," Bennet roared to his men. When we were alone, his dark eyes focused on me. "I will enjoy taking them."

"Good luck with that," I snarled.

"Every female can be tamed. I look forward to proving that to you, especially when they bring me your mate. She will be a true delight."

Shifter

He had no idea. Skye was not a female to tangle with, as he would soon learn. Her daughters were no less dangerous. "You will not have any of them," I warned, meaning every word.

He simply laughed, leaving the room and closing the door behind him.

Chapter 25

-Zebastian-

AS SOON AS WE LEFT Father's territory, I pulled out my phone and dialed Gabrihen.

"Yeah," he answered.

"My father's clans are on board. What's the plan?"

"We're heading North in Arcadie's plane."

"There's a landing strip just north of my father's territory. We'll meet you there."

"Better warn him we're coming."

"Knowing my father, he'll know about you before I reach him."

"Is he expecting us?"

"Yes. He understands the situation."

"See you in twenty."

I hung up and pocketed the phone. "Get ready to rock," I told Teak.

"We can't go through his territory," he warned.

"We're going around." I removed my clothes, stuffed them into a bag I could strap around my waist, and shifted to my wolf. My panther was faster, but it did not move

well with the bag flopping about. My wolf's wider girth kept the bag secure.

Teak made quick work at packing his things; he shifted into his eagle, and then grabbed his bag and took flight. Even he could not fly over my father's territory without raising alarm with Father's winged guards. Teak's association with me turned him into an outcast just like me. I wondered whether he missed his adopted father and family as much as I missed mine. It was something we would address soon enough, when all this drama panned out and I was free to go my own way.

My heart sank at that thought. Going my own way meant leaving Kaili behind, something I was not willing to do. She would not come with me, of course, nor would her father allow it. Drifting Spirians didn't live long, nor were they readily accepted into other clans. I could stay with Khalen's clan, learn from him. That, however, would mean my status would be too low for Kaili. Taking her as a mate when I was not in line for leadership would lower her status. Then again, Khalen did encourage me to take her innocence. Perhaps he knew it would pan into something more substantial? He had to have known about my bonding to her. Hell, every male in a fifty-mile radius would feel it, if not sense it.

Had Steed sensed it? I wondered. Was he planning to use her to get to me? What would he expect me to do? Did he know about our plans and our knowledge of Khalen's location? The questions fired from my thoughts like rounds through a machine gun as I loped through the woods, ignoring the pain from my injuries. Steed was a strategist, not a fighter. His gift was his mind and his ability to cast illusions. With a simple thought, he could get people to do what they never thought possible, only later to discover that it truly was impossible ... only now it was too late to reverse the actions.

By the time we reached the airport, the plane had landed and Father was talking to another man, large and regal in stature. His silver hair glistened in the sunlight, and his teeth were so bright that I could see them flashing in a smile from several yards away.

As I approached, my father growled, giving the stranger pause. I shifted, got dressed, then walked toward the men.

Gabrihen quickly intervened. "Arcadie, this is our good friend, Zebastian."

Good friend? Why had he felt it necessary to use that title? I stuck my hand out in greeting. "Arcadie." I bowed, showing my respect.

"I'm familiar with your name," he said, his voice deep and silky like a summer breeze. "Khalen has mentioned you numerous times."

That got a reaction from Father. He stood back, eyes wide, hands crossed over his broad chest.

"I fear I have caused him great trouble," I said, ignoring my father's discretion.

Arcadie laughed, the power of it reverberating off the trees. This man was powerful, more so than any Spirian I had ever met. Another man came to join us. He had darker hair, but resembled the older man in many ways.

"Case," said Arcadie, "this is Zebastian, the young man Khalen has touted."

The man's eyes lit up like phosphorus obsidian, radiating with colors of blue, red, yellow, and green. He nodded his head slightly while extending his hand. "Honor to meet such a fascinating young man."

Father walked away at that point, leaving the three

of us to get acquainted, without his presence. What was going through his mind? I wondered. His so called monster of a son had won the honor of Khalen's approval. That had to sting a bit.

Teak walked over and I introduced him to the two elders as more men gathered around—too many to fit into two planes. Father had air transport of his own, but it carried only a handful of men. The two planes the elders had flown in held maybe fifteen each.

Arcadie spoke, addressing the horde as if he owned them. What was even stranger was the immense respect he received from everyone, including my father. Who was this guy?

As if reading my mind, Gabrihen leaned in and whispered, "He is Skye's uncle, the eldest son of Shanuk."

"Skye carries Shanuk's blood?"

He scoffed. "She's his granddaughter. Case and Arcadie are his sons."

A chill ran down my spine as I realized I had touched the hands of the most powerful Spirians, of whom only legends had spoken. For years, I had believed that the great Shanuk was a figment of someone's over-active imagination, conjured to frighten and intrigue the young and old alike. Now here I was mingling with the horde that carried his blood. Kaili carried his blood, I suddenly realized. Why in God's good graces would Khalen ever ask him, a lowly son who had been cast out of his clan, to take her innocence? That would be akin to asking a pauper to escort a princess. It was simply unheard of.

"Listen up, people," Arcadie announced. "We prepare to face off with a Shadow who has clearly crossed the line. As I understand it, he has created an army of super shifters, those who don't feel pain and have thrice the strength of a normal Spirian. We have seen evidence of their strength in Uig and Brazil as our clans have been the target of their attacks." His sapphire eyes focused on me. "Zebastian knows a bit about these creatures. I would ask him to come forth and offer his insight."

I stepped forward, feeling like an ant at an aardvark convention. The eyes that set upon me were those of warriors awaiting information they could use. I cleared my throat and tried to ignore my father's disapproving stare.

"These super shifters have been altered to feel no pain, as Arcadie mentioned. They are also immune to illusions, energy bending and blasts. To take them down, you must outsmart them. Most were raised in sheltered environments and are not worldly, so outthinking them should not be too difficult. They were taught to fight with brawn and resilience, nothing more. Attack with fatal accuracy, and you will survive. Falter beneath their strength, and you will perish."

Arcadie nodded and smiled. "Thank you, Zebastian." He turned to address the crowd. "We take a third of you with us. The rest remain with Teak who will lead you to the mansions where these shifters are held as prisoners. No shifters will be harmed unless they threaten your life; understood?"

"Aye!" the crowd yelled.

He looked at my father, and bowed his head with respect, an act that was not expected or necessary. "Tiban, thank you for your support. You honor the clans as does your son."

Tiban's eyes glowed blue like the moon on a stormy night. He nodded back to Arcadie. "The honor is mine."

"Choose who will come with us and who will help Teak

destroy the mansions. We must act quickly. If Bennet discovers our numbers, he will call in reinforcements."

Tiban nodded, then left to talk with his clan. Funny how the men I had known at a young age no longer felt like my clan. I had been gone too long. Our connection had been severed by my father. I looked over at Gabrihen, Ian, Aidan, and the others. They were my clan now; a strange admission that had me feeling satisfied. Despite my father's severance of me, I still loved and respected the man; my mother, I sorely missed. I supposed the female I had been promised had been given to another, though to whom I could not even guess. She was a gentle bird, raised to obey her mate; not at all like Kaili who was spirited as the storm-driven wind.

I closed my eyes, willing my soul to reach out, find Kaili, and assure her I was coming. This would all end soon. What came back was an emptiness that hollowed my soul.

"Tame your thoughts," Arcadie whispered, "lest they rule you with darkness you cannot control."

When I looked over at him, he was too far away to have spoken to me. He smiled. The man's telepathic skills were impressive. I could have sworn he had been right here beside me, speaking the words to my ears.

"Are you ready for this?" asked Teak.

"I am, and you?"

"I've been praying for this day, my friend, since the moment those Shadow bastards took you from us."

"Let's do this, then."

~ Steed ~

I WALKED INTO BENNET'S OFFICE, KNOWING he would soon have my nuts on his wall, along with the other stuffed trophies he held so proud.

"Report," he drawled out, as if bored with the conversation already.

"The shifter was not with the clan."

"Then why do you stand here before me?"

"Because I believe he's on his way here—to find you."

That got his attention. He spun in his deep leather chair to face me. "Explain."

"The girl, Kaili—he's bonded with her."

The smile that stretched over his hard face left a sparkle in his eye. "Has he now? Bring the female to me."

I bowed, trying to hide my smile. "Sir."

Chapter 27

-Zebastian-

WHY MY FATHER CHOSE TO ride with me in Arcadie's plane was a mystery. He did not meet my eyes and seemed to be calm and meditative at the moment. It was his way before going into battle. His moods used to drive my mother mad with rage when he would not speak or acknowledge her presence days before a war. He just sat like a cold statue, indifferent to the conversations around him.

"Zebastian," Arcadie called out over his shoulder from the pilot's seat. "Come, sit with me."

I hadn't noticed that Aidan had given up his seat up front to join the rest of us crammed in the belly of the plane. I was sure we were over our weight limit. That the plane managed to leave the ground was nothing short of a miracle. Clambering past the men sitting upon the floor, I made my way to the vacant seat.

Arcadie studied me with those electrifying blue eyes, and then he flashed a smile that belonged to a Pepsodent model. "Khalen tells me you are a reaper."

"A gift that is new to me."

"Khalen does not become intrigued easily, but he is with you."

"I fear he wastes his time and effort then."

Arcadie laughed as if amused. "Khalen is not one to waste anything, especially time and effort. He sees great things in you; something I respect."

"My father does not feel the same."

"Your father is old school and sheltered from the changing times."

"He is not wrong about me. The Shadows changed who I am in those prisons. I have become the monster he claims me to be."

That invoked a frown from the elder. "Shame that you think so."

"Explain."

He trained his eyes before him, staring out at the vast blue that spread across the sky, broken only by sparse clouds. "What you believe is what you become, young man."

Did I believe I was a monster—really believe? "I lose myself in rage," I blurted, almost as if the words were a flame in me desperate to escape.

"Do you now?"

"When the rage sets in, I forget all things that occur during those moments and have no conscious thought. I'm dangerous."

"Aidan describes you otherwise."

I remembered how I had defeated the super shifters at the cabin, yet none of Khalen's clan members were injured. "It is something I cannot control."

"There are many things in life we cannot control, Zebastian. Do not disillusion yourself with that. Integrity is what reveals your soul and its truth. You have proven to be faithful, true to your word, and reliable where it counts. The rest is merely a product of life, nothing more."

"Convince my father of that."

"He will learn the truth of things in due time. Tiban is a good man, though stubborn to a fault."

Silence stretched between us before he steered the conversation into a new direction. "I understand you've bonded with my niece."

"I have."

"Yet you are not happy about it?"

"I would have something to offer her before feeling glad for it."

"I agree. Khalen will not let his daughter go to just any man. You will have to earn your right to claim her."

"For now, I'd be satisfied with freeing them from Bennet's grip."

"You sound doubtful."

Closing my eyes, I forced my aching jaw to relax. "I fear I have placed her in danger."

"Because Bennet has her?"

"My bonding scent surrounds her. That alone would entice that bastard's desire to claim her before me. If not, he will use her to get to me."

His eyes grew distant with thought. "Yes, that would fit his M.O. to a tee."

"Suggestions?"

"It might benefit us all if you were to surrender to him."

Had I heard him correctly? Was he out of his mind? "In what way?"

"Approach his fortress alone. Let him think he has won and holds the cards of worth. He will try to own you, of course, and will use Kaili to break you, but you must be strong. Use the advantage to learn Khalen's location and that of his daughters."

It was a sound plan. "He will become distracted with me while the rest of you move in."

"Exactly." I watched in fascination as he rotated a large wheel to his right and began our descent. "When we land, I will connect you to the clan. This will enable you to communicate with us over a distance."

My stiffness did not escape his notice.

"This concerns you?"

When I didn't answer, he cocked his head, eyes narrowed, mouth pursed. "You do not wish to be connected? Or perhaps you fear being ousted by Khalen?"

He voiced incomprehensible words into the microphone that connected to the earpiece he wore, flipped a few switches, and then turned the yoke in his hands to the left.

"Fear not," he said, operating the controls as if he had done this for hundreds of years. "Your will is still your own, Zebastian. Khalen will respect your decisions whatever they will be. Your connection to the clan is not binding."

Wasn't that the truth of all things? Nothing lasted forever, and the only certainty in life was your imminent death. I glanced back at my father, who stared out the window as if willing the wind to obey his command.

"You feel as if you abandon your father by connecting to our clan?"

The man's gifts knew no bounds. I had shielded my thoughts. Arrogant to think I could do so from this elder of Shanuk's blood. "You read me correctly."

"You do not give up one for the other. By connecting

to us, your father's clan grows stronger."

"He will see it as seditious."

"Perhaps, but that is more his issue, is it not?"

The discussion ended as his concentration turned to setting the plane down. In a sense, I was grateful. He read me so thoroughly it left me feeling violated. The man had peered into my soul and extracted a truth I kept hidden behind the steel guards of my heart. What else had he seen? I wondered. The pathetic weakness of my doubts was not exactly a badge I wore with pride.

As we stepped from the plane, he exited behind me. Before I knew what had happened, he had spun me around, gripped my hands with his, and formed the connection that would enable us to communicate over distances.

Replace your doubts with a better truth, he said to me telepathically. The words were as strong and clear as if he had spoken them into my ear.

The formal connection did not evade my father's notice. His eyes narrowed and his broad shoulders seemed to spread and rise like an eagle taking flight ... a warning. My future had just become a gauntlet through which I had to survive. Meeting his gaze, I raised my chin up a notch, showing him that I had acknowledged his signal and was standing my ground. Kaili's life was in danger and Arcadie's plan was a sound one.

When he announced the stratagem to the others, murmurs spread throughout the men, ceasing quickly when he raised his hand. Arcadie looked past the crowd to the two approaching figures.

Gabrihen kept pace with the older wizard he had called his mentor. The crowed parted as they came forth, both of them looking as if their team had lost the Super

Bowl.

"Report," said Arcadie.

The old wizard cleared his throat. "This fortress," he said, producing a holographic image of the island, "is not the work of Bennet Graves."

"Explain."

"It is the manifestation of Basalt."

"Basalt?"

"Son of Baru."

Arcadie's complexion paled as if he had eaten something foul. "Bloody perfect."

The young man named Connor stepped forward. "If you get me inside, I can change the properties of the manifestation."

Arcadie's head snapped around as if the young man had just slapped his backside with a wet towel. "How is this possible?"

It was Gabrihen who spoke. "He's an alchemist, Uncle."

The elder looked surprised for a moment, and then eased. "Of course. He's the son of Avel. I had not heard that he had come into his own."

"Khalen just learned of it."

"Yet you have known for quite some time, yes?"

Gabrihen shuffled a bit but his eyes met the leader's with resolve.

Connor cut in with, "I have only been able to alchemize substances on a small scale."

"Yet you think you can manipulate a manifestation of a fourth-generation wizard?"

His chin rose as he met the leader's gaze. "I do."

Tetris laughed. "The lad's the definition of cocky."

"More like suicidal," said Arcadie.

"I am the son of a Spartan warrior." The boy's voice deepened an octave, his cornflower-blue eyes hardening with misplaced wisdom.

Tetris stepped back, eyeing the youngster with new respect. "That ye are, young man, but you are untrained."

Arcadie looked between the old wizard and Gabrihen. "Can you pop him in?"

"Gettin' him in is not the problem. The walls could be lined in lead. We could be ambushed once inside. Bassalt is sure to have wards up, if not Bennet. Our presence will be known either way."

"Are you losing your nerve, old man?"

Tetris scoffed. "Losin' my nerve. Bollocks! I'm thinking of the lads; that's all. If anything happens to them, Khalen will have my head on a platter."

"Father will understand," said Gabrihen. "It's a sound plan."

Connor knelt down and started drawing symbols in the dirt. When talking ceased and every eye drew down upon him, he stood and used a long stick to point at various symbols. "If we enter here, I can start a chain reaction, changing the properties of the structure and everything inside. That will inhibit the wards as well. If we are fast enough, the change won't be detected."

"You say you've never done this before?" asked Arcadie.

"I see the alchemical structure of things. With a thought, I can change that structure simply by replacing one element with another." Focusing on Arcadie's shirt, he changed the fine silk into cotton, and then into gold before changing it back to silk.

"Fascinating," Arcadie said.

"I've studied Khalen's wards. They operate by sensing energy. When a sudden flux of energy occurs, the wards are triggered, sending a pulse toward the offender."

Arcadie stood back, his hand perched upon his chin as if pondering the young man's theory. Tetris listened with intent, his silver eyes glistening through narrowed slits. Gabrihen just smiled.

"By changing the structure and those of its wards, our energy will simply be absorbed and not reflected."

"How old are you?" asked Tetris.

"Fifteen; why?"

"Very impressive, young man," said Arcadie. "I can see why the Angels were so intent on your survival."

"You knew my father, then?"

"Aye; I battled beside the man."

"Did he have these skills?"

"The man was a spirit, but not of Spirian blood. His father Hermes was the father of alchemy, though, and had passed that knowledge on to his son, just as he has passed it on to you."

"He was a spirit of a human then, yes?"

"He was."

"So I am not full Spirian?"

Case intervened. "Is it wise to stand here for so long when my son is in danger?"

Arcadie turned back to Connor. "We'll discuss this further at another time, yes?"

The boy nodded.

Case's obsidian gaze fell upon me. "Ready yourself, Zebastian. You're about to enter the tiger's cage with a chunk of steak around your neck."

Chapter 28

~Zebastian~

THERE I STOOD ON THE deck two miles from the island that would soon become my prison should our plans fall short. It wouldn't take long for Bennet to know of my presence.

Moments later, a Zodiac motorboat with four men cruised up, sending a lofty wake as it docked. One man hopped onto the deck and approached me, holding out a collar. "You are to wear this," he said in a Scottish accent. His facial hair was so thick and black, he resembled a bear.

"No, I won't."

Another man approached, holding a taser in his hand.

"I offer myself willingly. There is no need for restraints."

"Don the collar, ye lousy cur, or suffer the consequences."

I still bore scars from the last collar that marked me as a prisoner. I wasn't too eager to don one again. The other two men secured the boat before joining the others. I could defeat them, but that would defeat my purpose. Having no choice, I snatched the dangled collar from the

Shifter

Scot's hand. They smelled of fear, no doubt warned of my ... abilities. I wrapped the collar around my neck, wincing as the collar snapped together, the tiny probes puncturing my skin.

"Very well, then. Come. We are to escort you," taser man said.

The boat swayed beneath me as I stepped into its belly. The Scot fell in behind me, followed by taser man. The other two stayed perched on the dock. They nodded as if following a silent command.

After the ropes were freed, the Scot rotated the motor and drove the boat from the dock, accelerating as the distance between land and us increased. Every instinct screamed this was a bad idea ... an insane idea. Wearing this cursed collar, I had no chance of saving Kaili and her family. I had become a pawn sent to kill Khalen, or worse. What could I do if Bennet hurt Kaili in front of me? Tethered, like this, I could do nothing to stop him. My eyes would witness her pain, my soul would tear at my chest, demanding retribution. Worse yet, my communication with the clan was severed.

With practiced efficiency, the Scot docked the boat while his buddy secured the ropes. Being twice their size, they refrained from hauling me out of the boat. Already, they granted me a wide berth between them as we marched up the dock toward the dismal stone fortress. I watched as they punched in a few numbers on the keypad before holding some sort of card to a flat black panel. The light above it flashed green three times, and locks that rivaled those of a bank vault rumbled and groaned as they slid aside.

Through a narrow tunnel, the Scot led the way while taser man sandwiched me between them, keeping a safe distance—smart man. Even collared, I could make quick work of him before the shock disabled me. Lights flickered as we made our way through the dark and dank labyrinth of tunnels that ended at stairs. We climbed them.

"Where does that lead?" I asked, gesturing to the wider hall to our left.

Taser man shoved me forward. "None of your business."

I stopped short, causing him to run into me. One look at my eyes had him stumbling back like a rat from a striking snake. My wolf had been invoked, no doubt causing my irises to expand, along with my pupils. My added growl prompted him to increase the distance between us.

With shaking hands, he held the taser before him. "Move it, or I'll zap you."

"You intend to carry me up these stairs, then?"

"Leave it," the Scot grumbled over his shoulder. "We're nearly there."

Five flights of stairs and seven corridors later, we arrived at a set of eight-foot high French doors constructed of teak, hand-carved by the looks of them. They opened, revealing a huge room with a desk, an impressive view of the ocean, and a well-stocked bar. A tall man smiled over at us as we entered the room. He looked at the two blokes escorting me. "Leave us." The door closed behind them, moved by the man's will. His smile lingered as he looked me up and down. "Zebastian Carue," he drawled as if seducing the name with his tongue.

"Bennet Graves, I presume?"

He was a handsome man with peppered hair, steely eyes, and a stature that demonstrated his power and confidence. Though shorter than me, he carried himself well and looked to be in good shape. The power that radiated around him hummed like a well-tuned engine at full throttle.

"Correct. You, however, will call me ... Master."

"And why would I do that?"

He walked over and fingered the collar around my neck. "Because I created you and command you."

"Then you have made a grave error because your creation will be your undoing."

"I don't think so."

We're in, I heard a voice chime in my mind. It was Tetris. Connor must have altered the fortress' structure and contents as promised, or else the collar would have prevented the communication.

I'm with Bennet, I replied, making sure to keep my thoughts from the leader standing before me. If he knew about the infiltration, he could scan my thoughts. Under the illusion of the collar's restriction, however, he had no reason to try.

"Where is Khalen and his daughters?" I asked, knowing it would open his thoughts to me. That enabled me to glean information about their location, in theory anyway. His mind was impenetrable, locked tighter than a waterproof vessel.

"Their location is not your concern." He went on to make idle threats and empty boasts, which I ignored for the moment.

Khalen, we're here. Where are you?

With Shaiya. Bennet has taken Kaili. She must be incapacitated. I cannot reach her. Remain silent lest Bennet tap your thoughts.

He had a good point. I did not reply. Expanding my senses, I reached out to locate my mate. Though not united, I still had the bonding instinct that enabled me to sense her. She was close.

Bennet's expression fell as if he felt something unexpected. My reaching out to Kaili must have triggered his instincts—stupid thing to do, I feared.

He lifted the receiver on the phone and pressed a button. "Alert security and release the shifters." He hung up, the concern etching his features like water through a canyon. "I was hoping to do this a different way."

I watched as he walked with purpose toward a closed door. When he opened it, Kaili lay on a couch, unconscious. The bruises on her face had my blood boiling to the point where Bennet would soon end up hashed to a bloody pulp.

"Think about this, Zebastian. I could drop you like a rag doll before your rage gains power."

"What do you want?" My voice sounded more monstrous than human.

Bennet smiled. "Unfortunately, my walls have been breached as you know, so my plans are altered."

"Kaili, wake up!"

God, I needed her now, needed to hear her voice in my head. I prayed she was all right and that the bastard hadn't touched her, or worse, claimed her.

Bennet must have tapped my thoughts. His laugh grated my nerves like nails on a chalkboard. "I would have if she hadn't passed out. I thought to claim her before you as you watched, but she proved weaker than expected. She collapsed after a single blow. Quite disappointing, I assure you."

Kaili? Collapsed after one blow? Unlikely. Yet her thoughts remained silent. Knowing that animal communication reached further and deeper into the mind, I reached out to her with my wolf thoughts. *Kaili, I'm here. Wake up.*

Images from her scattered mind flooded my thoughts. She'd heard me and was stirring. *That's it, love. Come back to me now.*

Ze, he's—.

The door crashed open, wood splinters scattered like shards of glass through the air. Beyond them stood a dozen super shifters hungering for my blood. Bennet needed me occupied while he carried Kaili away. He counted on my rage to blind me. Not this time. Ripping the collar from my neck, I shifted into my wolf, powerful, strong, and fast. Keeping my wits during battle presented a challenge I had never conquered before. Then again, I never had something so precious to protect. Kaili, I realized, was my life, my blood. Without her, my soul would have no purpose.

Not only did I have super shifters to battle, but I also had to keep Bennet from leaving the room with my female. The odds lay stacked in his favor. In a blur, a bear attacked, followed by a panther and a wolf, three of the most powerful shifters. It made sense, of course. For an army, you would want the most formidable creatures at your command. If my collar had been disarmed by Connor's alterations, the shifters' collars would be so as well. I wondered whether they knew.

Throwing the bear to the wall and scoring the cat with my claws, I reached out with my thoughts, letting them know they were now free. The wolf leaped toward my throat. I twisted and bit his ear. Were they not listening to me?

I heard Kaili's sweet thoughts over the din of growls and hisses. Claws and teeth raked my body, sinking deep into my flesh. I would not survive without my rage. The other beasts were chomping to engage, to join in with the final kill of my body. I continued to fight, twisting and clawing my attackers before they could gain fatal purchase on my flesh, but my strength faded.

Kaili's thoughts must have reached them, for their attacks slowed, their eyes softened.

You're free. Remove your collars.

One by one, they tore their collars from their necks and shifted back into human form.

Bennet tried to bind them with energy, but he could not cast it fast enough. He was strong, though, much stronger than the shifters with little training. They fell beneath his skill as I lay helpless in observation. Kaili, too, was bound, unable to move.

"Where the hell are my guards?" muttered Bennet.

"Dead," said a familiar voice in the doorway. Khalen stood with Arcadie, Case, and Aidan by his side. Khalen's eyes glowed so bright they rivaled the sun's intensity.

"Do you think you can defeat me?"

Khalen said nothing, but his thoughts were clear. *Get up. Together we can reap him.*

I'm bound.

Arcadie severed the bind surrounding Kaili and me. Still weak from battle and wounds, I stood on shaky legs.

"Arcadie," Bennet growled. "I'm going to enjoy taking you down."

"Cocky boast considering your company."

"My power extends beyond these walls. My territories are vast, my subjects loyal and fierce. They will avenge me."

Ready yourself, thought Khalen.

I had never reaped anyone outside of my rage, and I wasn't quite sure I could do it. He must have sensed my apprehension.

Focus!

I imagined Bennet's soul separate from his body. At that moment, he turned to face me.

"Now!" Khalen barked.

The intensity in the room was like a lightning storm, coupled with thunderous outburst and bone-shattering vibration. Bennet was strong, powerfully so. He held back our attack with impressive ease. That is until Arcadie added his own power. Bennet shattered like frozen lead dropped on granite. Aidan chimed in, turning Bennet's spent body into white ash.

Kaili rushed over to me, intent on hugging me fiercely. My shredded body stopped her as wild green eyes scanned me from head to toe.

"Zebastian?"

"I'm fine."

Horrid screeches echoed off the stone walls as if hell had been released.

"It's not over," said Arcadie. "Khalen, get the girls out of here, now!"

Khalen reached over and grabbed Kaili's arms. In a blink, they were gone.

"Can you fight?" Arcadie asked me.

I nodded, gathering the strength I would need to see this through.

Chapter 29

~Kaili~

BACK AT THE PLANE WITH my father and sister, I paced like a caged lion. Where were the others? Why hadn't we heard from them?

"Kaili, relax," said Shaiya.

"Ze is injured and should have returned with us. Why did Arcadie ask him to stay?"

My father was beside himself as well. He'd been trying to contact Mum with no success. I heard him growl several times. When his head snapped up, I knew the clan had contacted him.

"What is it?" I asked.

"They're on their way." He looked over at Shaiya. "How are your healing skills?"

She paled. "Weak compared to Mum's. Why? Who's injured?"

He didn't need to speak the name; the look he gave me was answer enough.

"Several," he said. "Damn it! Where's Skye?"

Our mum had a way of finding trouble, especially

when her family was in danger. She had the spirit to join them if it were an option. Not even Ian and Aidan had the strength to stop her and that was a problem.

It seemed to take eons for the clan to arrive. When they did, their bloodied bodies looked to have endured a tornado. Their clothing hung in scraps; their faces were swollen, covered in bruises and cuts. Even Arcadie was limping, his arm dripping with blood. Was it his or that of the person he carried, limp and naked? One look at the flopping hands and my heart ceased for several beats. On their own volition, my legs sprinted over the rocky ground.

"Zebastian!"

"Easy, lass," said Arcadie. "He's injured but alive."

Never in my life had I felt so helpless as when they lifted Ze's body into the plane. Shaiya placed shaky hands over his wounds, praying for the Father's help.

"Can you save him?" I asked, wishing for the first time that I possessed the skill to heal.

"I'll try."

Needing something to occupy my mind, I helped the others load into the plane.

"Bring them to my home," said Tiban. "We have supplies there and a healer."

When our plane was full, Arcadie hobbled to the pilot's seat and fumbled with the headset and safety harness. I offered a hand.

"Thank you, lass."

His right arm bent at an odd angle, broken at the wrist. How had he managed to carry Zebastian back from the boat? It was at least a mile away.

"Can I help?"

"Send your father up here."

I nodded, then left to find him loading the last few injured into Tiban's plane.

"Arcadie needs you," I told him.

"Ride with them," he said, gesturing to Tiban's plane.

"I want to stay with Ze."

"It's best you don't."

"Why? I need to know—"

"The ride is a short one and there are plenty here who can use a hand."

He was right, of course. There was nothing I could do for Zebastian now. Shaiya was his best hope, not me. "Okay."

He smiled down at me and squeezed my hand. "He'll be fine." The dullness in his eyes looked foreign to me. He must be worried sick about Mum; we all were. He waited for me to enter the plane before jogging back to Arcadie.

One of Tiban's men shoved a rag in my hand. "Apply pressure to his leg." He pointed to a young man with a gash in his thigh. Without hesitation, I knelt beside the shifter and pressed the rag to his wound. Having assisted Ian and Aidan at the vet clinic for several years, I had a stomach for this. To calm the young man, I spoke to his cougar in a calm, soothing tone. His breathing slowed as he studied me with nocturnal eyes.

"You belong to Ze," he mumbled, drawing the attention of those on the plane. I felt Tiban's energy spike and his eyes grow cold.

"I do," I said, making sure the leader heard me.

The plane rumbled over the dirt path that had served as a makeshift runway. From the passenger's seat up front, Tiban studied me with such intensity that I could feel him all around me.

"Do you know what he is?" he asked.

I met his blue-gray eyes, deep and knowing like his son's. "I do."

"Then perhaps you're blind as your mother?"

That heated my blood a few degrees. "You speak as if you know nothing about her ... because if you did, you would not speak so carelessly."

He laughed at that. "Do not think that because you are Khalen's daughter you can wag your tongue so loosely, child."

"And who are you to wag yours with such abandon and ignorance?"

He stood, his face red now and his jaw clenched so tight it drew bands across his cheeks. With a wave of his hand, the energy he projected tossed me hard against the wall. Blood trickled from my scalp down my neck.

"Tiban," an older man said. "Perhaps this is not the time or place?" Where had he come from? I wondered. I didn't remember seeing him before. He had not joined in the battle, or if he did, he endured the ordeal without a single cut or scrape.

"Your father will hear of this," Tiban growled at me.

"I fight my own battles."

Probing his thoughts and animal spirit, I gained information he would not volunteer. His feelings toward Zebastian made sense now. Tiban came from an abusive home, rising to leadership through pain and strife. Perhaps he intended the same for Ze?

"I find your insolence disturbing."

"Good thing this plane ride is short then, yes?"

"You shame your bloodline with such rebellion."

"And you shame yours with ignorance."

This time, his energy blast hit me with precision, holding me in place as if spikes had been driven through my flesh. I did not give him the satisfaction of hearing my cries, though they pressed to the surface of my control.

"Stay quiet, child," the older man hissed. "Do you not know the company you keep?"

I did know. Shifters were a different breed of Spirians, which was why they kept to themselves. This old man, however, was not a shifter. The fury and temper in shifters were quick to spark and their physical strength surpassed that of most leaders. Perhaps angering Tiban was not a wise strategy.

"I would hear your apologies," he said.

Damn my pride, it gripped my tongue with a death hold and laced it with poison as I replied, "Why? Your ignorance is not my doing."

More pain. A smart female would call out to my father by now, but my pride stood firm in its position.

Kaili, my father thought to me. *Zebastian is going berserk. Calm him.*

If I reached out to Ze now, he would know about my pain and his father's hand in it.

Too late, my father had opened that telepathic window. Ze knew my predicament. My father did too. Hell was about to gain purchase.

Tiban's cell phone rang. He answered it with a smile that quickly faded.

"I will not! Her tongue has no respect. She speaks like a misfit with no proper training."

I felt my father's wall of protection wrap around me and the pain subsided.

Ze, I reached out. *I'm all right.*

I will kill him for this, he replied.

No, this is my fight. I will handle it.

You are mine.

Then you know me well enough to disengage.

I felt his growl deep in my bones.

Returning to the young shifter, I applied pressure to his wounds. The glassy look in his eyes held compassion and a bit of fear. When I smiled, they softened a bit.

"I see what he likes in you."

The plane ride, though lasting only thirty minutes, seemed to stretch on for hours. When we landed, the energy in the air resembled that of a thunderstorm. Tiban charged from the plane with purpose. My father matched his stride. Arcadie, Case, and the old man in our plane quickly dashed between the two leaders.

"Nothing good will come of this," said Arcadie.

The older man gripped Tiban's shoulder, not budging when Tiban retaliated with a sharp swipe.

"Stop, Tiban! You do not think clearly now. Cool off and discuss this later with rational thought." With surprising force, the old man shoved Tiban away, his golden eyes glowing with warning. Not even the strongest of leaders would challenge an elder lest he become ash at the elder's feet.

Tiban shifted into a great black wolf and ran toward the woods.

My father's eyes fell upon me. "Explain."

"Tiban was out of line," said the old man. "She is innocent."

Well, that wasn't entirely correct, but who was I to argue? I nodded to the old man. "Thank you."

My father approached him, hand extended. "I don't believe we've met."

The old man gripped Father's hand with impressive strength. "No need, Khalen Dunning. Your reputation is well known in this region."

"Your name?"

When the old man smiled, his teeth reflected the sun like fresh-fallen snow. "Ren, son of Dukonu."

The names meant nothing to me, but the expressions reflected in Khalen, Case, and Arcadie's faces were that of awe and recognition.

Arcadie was the first to speak. "You're Shanuk's brother?"

"Younger brother, destined to grow in the perpetual height of his shadow."

"As we all are," said Case. "That would make you our uncle, then."

Ren nodded. "Come; the others have returned. My son and his horde were successful. You will be pleased with what they found."

Chapter 30

~Kaili~

DURING THE WALK FROM THE personal airstrip to the large camp that was more like a small city in the midst of woods, Arcadie told Khalen what had happened with Skye.

"We had to restrain her."

My father growled.

"Easy, lad. I'm not talking about tying her down. She insisted on breaking you and the girls out of that fortress and sending Bennet to an early grave. Anyone trying to stop her received an energy blast that rivaled a leader's. Christ, I've never know a female with that kind of strength. Even I struggled to suppress her."

"Where is she?"

"Safe in this camp. She's sedated. Ian placed her in an illusion that would not rouse her suspicion. Can't really predict how she'll react when he removes it."

My worst nightmare couldn't compare to that moment when Ian lifted the illusion. It was akin to freeing a bolt of lightning. The blast that radiated around my mother was enough to create a crater the size of a city block. If Father hadn't countered the blast, we'd be sitting in a field of rubble instead of a house.

"I'm here, love," he cooed. "We all are. Everything's all right."

My mother wrapped her arms around him so tightly I thought he would soon pass out from lack of oxygen. She shook as she touched his face and scanned his body for injuries. When they roamed over his chest, she shuddered.

"You're hurt!" It took nothing for her to heal him. They were connected in so many ways, she could knit his wounds from any distance.

After she was assured that my siblings and I were okay, she and Father got busy with healing the injured. I prayed it wasn't too late for Ze. He remained still, his breathing so shallow his chest didn't rise.

"He's lost a lot of blood," Mum said. "His arm and leg are broken along with several of his ribs."

"Internal bleeding in his abdomen," Father said. He looked over at the clan doctor who busied himself with triaging the others. "Have we any blood?"

"Yes, of course. On that tray over there along with the IV kits." He gestured to a cart on wheels.

"Kaili, bring me a kit and two pints of blood."

We didn't have to worry about blood type because Spirian blood was universal. Fetching what he needed, I busied my trembling hands with assembling the mess. When he was ready, I handed Father the tab end of the needle, a tourniquet, and a cotton ball drenched in alcohol. You didn't live with a surgeon without learning the basics of assisting.

"Stop the bleeding first," he told Mum.

"Shaiya healed most of the bleeders. An impressive

attempt, really." She eyed the bag. "Seth said giving Ze blood might send him into anaphylactic shock." She moved her hands over Ze's belly, then to his chest. After Father straightened Ze's broken limbs, she fused the bones together.

"If we don't give it to him, he'll die."

She glanced up at me. "He'll be fine."

The entire process took less than a minute. They made a powerful team. It was then that I realized how truly magical a good union could be. Would Ze and I be that powerful? My thoughts of joining with him drew Father's attention. His lips grew firm as he clenched his teeth.

"You don't approve?" I asked him.

"You've never had time to explore. It's unnatural to settle for the first man to come about."

"He's bonded with me."

"An obvious fact."

"I want him as well."

Snapping on a fresh pair of gloves, he moved to the next victim—the young man I had aided in the plane. "Fetch me another blood kit."

Mum stood and followed me over. "He wants the best for you is all."

"I thought he liked Ze."

"He does. He's just not ready to give you up to your first suitor."

"Kaili!" he snapped.

Nothing shadowed my father's foul moods. When he was unhappy, he shared the emotion with everyone around him. I used to be able to calm his thoughts. Today, I only served to exasperate them. I made quick work of preparing the kit before handing it over.

Mum healed the wound as Father inserted the IV.

"Tend to the others," he told me. "There is much to be done."

"Yes sir." I knew he didn't mean to be so harsh. The stress of the day had caught up to him. He had reaped many lives and stood drained. I could see it in his eyes. It must be taking everything he had to keep going. Placing a hand on his shoulder, I said, "I love you."

He reached up and squeezed my hand. "I'm sorry for being short. We'll discuss this later, yes?"

"Of course."

Mum smiled up at me as I left to assess the needs of the others. Next to those who needed blood, I prepared and laid IV kits. I then moved to clean wounds, bandage injuries, and fetch food and water for those who were able to eat and drink. By the time the lot was stable and resting, I felt ready to collapse. My clothes stained with blood, I was ready for a shower. As I walked out of the temporary trauma center, I found my sister pressing an accusatory finger against Teak's chest.

"You're Ren's son? We're related?"

Before Teak could answer, she continued with, "God. We had sex together. That's incest!"

He gripped her hand. "I'm not his son by birth. Relax."

Shaiya's eyes narrowed at me as I scooted past. "What are you smiling at?"

"Looks like love," I said.

For once, Shaiya, my over-exuberant twin, had no reply. She just looked at me with wide eyes, her mouth hung open as if the words she intended to express were caught in her throat.

Moving on, I added, "It's all right. It was destined to happen sooner or later."

"Not lo—"

Her words choked when Teak grabbed her and planted a kiss on her mouth.

Someone entered the room.

"Zhentu?" God, yes, it was him. He was older now, and ripped with muscle. Soft blond facial hair covered his chin, but his eyes had not changed. They were that same shade of silver gray as our mum's. Arms spread wide, I ran toward him, eager to feel him against me once again. It had been far too long.

He embraced me, crushing my body to his as if releasing it would mean forever. "Hey, sis. You've filled out some, yeah?"

I stood back, wanting to drink him in with renewed eyes. "You too. You're taller than me now."

"A lot has changed." Even his voice had grown deeper. There was weariness there where once had been endless energy.

Shaiya wrapped her arms around him and tried to swing him about like she used to. He didn't budge. "A bit heavier now," she groaned.

He picked her up and spun her around, instead. "It's good to see you."

The three of us stood there, staring at each other as if embedding memories that would never fade. As tears pooled in my eyes, all I could do was hold him once again. Shaiya joined in and we remained that way for a moment.

Gabrihen, Mum, and Father came sprinting toward us, eyes wide and disbelieving. Not surprisingly, Mum reached him first, covering the young man in kisses and tears. The fortunate soul remained buried among hugs and kisses for quite some time.

"Did you guys miss me?" he teased.

Whatever tension and exhaustion had plagued my

father before vanished in the light of this miracle. Zhentu was back.

Father stepped back, eyes drawn with speculation as he scanned the boy from head to toe.

"What is it?" asked Mum.

"He's been chipped."

Chapter 31

~Kaili~

As Father had suspected, all the shifters were chipped and, no doubt, tracked to this location. The camp was in danger.

"We must remove them," said Father.

"And destroy them," added Gabrihen.

"No," said Father. "We will gather them up. If the Shadows are tracking their signals, we'll draw them to a location that serves our advantage."

"They will know," a familiar voice sounded from the doorway. I turned to see Zebastian standing on shaky legs.

I ran toward him, and then slowed. There was a distance in his eyes I hadn't noticed before. "Ze?"

He pulled me to him and gently kissed the top of my head.

"Explain," said Father.

"The chips are designed to explode when removed from the body."

"Yet you removed yours?"

His right chest sported a sunken cavity where the chip

had been torn from his flesh.

"Thrown at my captors to aid my escape. I could not run fast enough to evade injury. If my body had not been pumped with serum, I would not be standing before you today."

"How do the chips work?"

Feeling Ze's strength ebb, I urged him over to a chair. He refused to let me go, his trembling hand wrapped tight around my own.

"I'm not sure. They are different than the one you found in me. I suspect they are triggered by sudden changes of temperature."

Father rubbed his forehead as if staving off a headache. Once again, he looked ready to collapse. His exhaustion did not escape my mother's notice. The furrow of her brow marked her concern. Unfortunately, after healing so many injuries, she had little left of herself to offer him. Still, her delicate hands rested upon his shoulders, offering comfort.

"Perhaps Connor could help?" All heads turned to Gabrihen.

"In what manner?" asked Father, his voice shaky and faltering.

"He can alter the walls, turn them to lead. It would prevent the Shadows from tracking the shifters until we have time to rest." His eyes settled on Father.

"A sound plan," he said. "I'll summon him."

Connor came quickly, despite the injuries he had endured in battle. Knowing him, he enjoyed the fight and was now pumped by it. Eyes bright, he spotted Zhentu and offered a bone-crushing hug.

"Lord, you've grown."

"As did you," Zhentu replied. "It's good to see you."

Gabrihen interrupted the reunion by placing a hand on Connor's shoulder. "We need you to do something."

Connor's eyes roamed between us, growing dim with concern. "What is it?"

"The shifters, Zhentu included, have been chipped. Can you change the walls of the infirmary to lead?"

"Of course."

"Get everyone inside the room," said Father. His eyes dimmed as they looked over at Zhentu. Imprisoning him yet again shortly after regaining his freedom seemed sacrilegious. Father must have felt the same way.

"It'll be all right," Zhentu assured him. "It's' temporary."

"Aye, temporary."

After Father explained the reasons to Tiban and his clan, Connor was given the cue to impart his unique blend of magic.

"It is done," he announced a few moments later.

"It looks the same," said Father.

"These walls are thick with insulation and the structure is sound. I changed the insulation to lead, offering greater protection."

"Are you sure it worked?"

Cocky as Connor was, he looked shocked at Father's doubt. "Only one way to find out. Step inside and try to invoke your gifts."

Father did just that, needing his own kind of reassurance. Too much was at risk not to. When he returned, his black expression was proof enough.

"Convinced?" asked Connor, smiling as if already knowing the answer.

"Bloody amazing," Father said. "It is a useful gift you have."

More amazing was how Connor's smile managed to

boast further pride. He would be impossible to live with now.

"It is time to rest," said Mum. "There is food in the commons room if you are hungry. I'm taking your father to bed."

"Good idea," I said. "For all of us."

"Stay alert," said Father. "I have a bad feeling."

WE AWOKE TO THE BLARING sound of an alarm, cutting through the early morning hours like acid through silk. Zebastian rolled on top of me, his eyes darting about.

"What is that?" I asked.

"The camp is under attack."

He jumped from the bed and looked out the window. "Get down to the basement." Shifting into his wolf form, he sprinted out of the room.

I had to find my mother and sister. As I dressed quickly, the din outside rolled like thunder against the windows. Shadows closed in with hordes of shifters. There must have been over a hundred of them. Tiban's clan was large, but not enough to ward against this intrusion. Without help, we would be overtaken; something I would not stand by to watch.

Whatever you're thinking, thought Zebastian. *Forget it. Stay inside with the women.*

The ridiculous request didn't merit a reply.

The house was in chaos, people running everywhere. The infirmary door was open, the shifters gone. Women barked orders as they gathered the children. Where were my mother and sister?

Their rooms were empty. *Mum, Shaiya.*

Get to the basement, my mother replied.

They were safe. Thank God.

A male tiger crashed through the window, snagging a young boy. Without thought, I lunged toward them, dislodging the boy's arm from the tiger's mouth.

"Run!" I told the young.

The tiger snarled, its golden eyes flashing fear and anger. Using my calming thoughts, I spoke to it, trying to ease his confusion and pain.

He shook his massive head as if trying to free his ears from pesky flies. Then, with a roar, he charged me, teeth bared and claws extended. I darted to the side, barely escaping his paw. Another attack followed. I rolled to my back, kicking the animal's tender belly as it flew on past. It roared in pain but quickly recovered. My thoughts had no effect on his mind. The creature fought, blinded by madness.

More shifters came in his wake, tearing apart the furniture and anything else in their path. Temporarily distracted by their presence, the Tiger looked away long enough for me to grab a lantern. I tore off the shade and jabbed the bulb end of the lantern into the tiger's side. The animal twisted and jolted, eyes wide, mouth frothing as electricity coursed through his flesh. I dropped the fixture and slowly backed away, not wanting to attract the attention of the others.

Predators hunted and tracked by movement. Remaining still was my best hope for surviving this mess—or so I thought. A Shadow grabbed a handful of my hair, pulling me back against him.

Shifter

~Zebastian~

STUBBORN FEMALE. **S**HE WOULD GET herself killed. Did she not understand the power of these beasts? Fighting my way through Shadows and super shifters, I made my way toward the house. There I saw my brave Kaili stab a tiger with a lamp—clever girl. When I saw the Shadow who dared to hold her to him, my protective instincts slammed into overdrive and my rage clung on the edge. Not yet, I told myself. Kaili could get hurt in the wake.

"Let her go," I told the Shadow.

Like a fool, he laughed, running his tongue along her neck. Kaili twisted, grabbed the man's hand and twisted it into an odd angle. He screamed. She rammed her knee into his face again and again until he collapsed at her feet.

Stupid of me to think she couldn't defend herself. Had I not seen her in action before? It was too late to get her to the safety of the basement. The place was flooded with the enemy, intent on vengeance for their fallen leader.

"Stay beside me," I told her.

She nodded, keeping her eyes trained on the encroaching horde. To survive this, I would have to unleash my rage.

"Let it go," she said, having read my thoughts. "I'll be all right."

Releasing the beast that resulted in an uncontrollable frenzy, my last thought was of her and praying the Angels would keep her safe from the demon I was about to become.

"THE BOY IS THE DEVIL," I heard my father say.

"He is a man," said Khalen. "One who saved your life and those of this entire clan."

"Your father forged your strength from the fires of hell," said Kaili. "Do not think your son any different."

"You speak out of place," roared Father.

"I speak the truth. Zebastian is the image of you. Do not cast him aside because you don't like the reflection."

As always, the rage left me disoriented and weak. This conversation between my father and mate would not end well. I could already feel the heat of energy build between them, yet I couldn't open my eyes, let alone save her from his wrath. If Khalen had not been present, I would have expended my last breath to save her. Damn my weakness.

"Your daughter shames you, Khalen, with her careless tongue."

"I back her on this," he said. "Zebastian fought well and suffered more than any man deserves. He is a son you should be proud of."

"Yet he chose to join your clan."

"A decision he did not make lightly. Say the word and he would return to you with heart and devotion."

"A foolish endeavor," Father said, storming out of the room.

"How many times can he survive this?" asked Kaili, her soft hand flowing over my forehead. "I feel his essence slip from this world as if my own soul withers."

"He is very weak and needs rest."

"I wish I could give him what Mum can give you."

"What makes you think you can't?"

"She is a healer. I'm not. My only gift is to talk to animals, a weak comparison to this man I love."

"Love is it?"

Silence. More than anything, I wanted to hear those sweet words from her lips again and again.

"Yes, I believe it is love; no other word describes this

hunger. I may not have much experience, Father, but I do know how my heart feels and what it wants."

Khalen sighed as if giving in to a truth that hung by a single fragile thread in the face of a tornado. "I respect your decision, but know this. Not even God, himself, will save this man should he hurt you in any way."

"Ze would never hurt me, Father, just as you could never lay harm to Mum."

"Aye, you might be right about that. My promise, however, still holds."

"A promise that will never need fulfillment," I struggled to say.

"Ze!" Kaili's arms folded around me like silk dipped in heat, soft and tender on my raw and battered skin.

"My angel," I said, kissing the side of her neck.

A knock sounded upon the door. Through blurry eyes, I could still recognize the figure of my mother. Her beautiful long red hair flowed over her shoulders, accenting the emerald eyes that shone beneath delicate brows.

"May I come in?"

"Of course," I said.

She made her way toward me. Kaili tried to stand, giving my mother room, but I held firm to her hand. "Stay with me."

"Mother, I'd like you to meet the female I intend to mate. This is Kaili, daughter of Khalen and Skye."

Khalen stiffened, looking as if holding his tongue were akin to sucking a hot pepper.

Mother, too, stood still, her tiny hands gathering the satin fabric of her gown—one that matched the shade of her eyes. She looked to Kaili and then to Khalen.

"Does your father know of this?"

"Yes."

"That certainly explains his foul mood."

Kaili met my mother's stare with equal fervor. "His foul mood does not come from the news of our union. It comes from his own shattered pride."

"Kaili!" said Khalen. "You forget yourself."

Mother smiled and extended her hand. "You must be the female he's been grumbling about. My name is Shinda."

"Pleasure to meet you."

Mother looked toward Khalen. "Will you excuse us a moment?"

Khalen cast his daughter a censured look before bowing his head and taking leave.

"I apologize for my outburst," she said, when Khalen walked out of earshot, rebellious to the end.

"No need. You speak the truth, something my mate needs to hear. God knows my words fall on deaf ears."

"He's a steadfast man."

Mother stifled a laugh. "A polite way to say he's stubborn as a grass stain."

I reached for her hand. "Things are tense between you?"

"Yes, since the day he sent you away. I feel more like a discarded shirt than his mate these days."

"He had his reasons."

"Justification can make a case for any wrongdoing, but it does not make it right by any measure."

"He believes I killed my brother."

She looked up and blinked a few times as if fighting a rancid emotion newly unearthed.

"Carter is dead. Nothing can change that now."

My father's wide frame filled the doorway, his gray

eyes fixed on my mother.

"Your assistance is needed in the infirmary," he told her, his voice stern and demanding.

She leaned down, kissing my forehead. "Rest now. We'll talk again soon." As she passed by my father, he released a low growl.

"You defy my wishes?"

"I see my son."

When he grabbed her arm, I swung my legs from the bed, nearly knocking Kaili off in the process. "Release her."

Mother shook her head at me. "No, Zebastian. Do not interfere."

My legs felt numb and trembled beneath my weight. Kaili tried to steady me.

"Release her."

"You dare challenge me?"

"I merely ask you to reconsider and direct your anger to one more worthy of it."

He shook his hand free of Mother's arm, leaving a red mark in its place. "This day is long coming."

"He is weak, Tiban. Can this not wait?" asked Mother, showing not a hint of fear.

"I believe I've had my fill of insolence. I will not tolerate it another minute." His eyes fell to me. "Apologize."

My legs finally gave in as I sank to the floor.

"Can you not see he's exhausted?" asked Kaili. "Leave now and let him rest."

Father strode through the door, reached down, and hauled me back to my feet. He then carried me back to the bed, letting me fall like a sack of grain.

"Do not challenge me again."

Chapter 32

~Zebastian~

KHALEN AND HIS CLAN STUCK around for another month to help restore the buildings damaged in the battle. They were due to leave on the morrow at first light. The question was, would I join them?

The sun fell below the horizon as we gathered in the commons room prepared to share the day's last meal. Khalen approached, looking far too serious for my comfort.

"May I have a word, Zebastian?"

Was this about my loyalties? I wondered. I followed him into the study where my father liked to enjoy a glass of brandy at day's end.

Khalen poured himself a glass of brandy and swirled it around a bit. "Would you like one?"

I was not a big fan of drinking; however, tonight it might do me some good. "Please."

Khalen handed me a snifter, clinked my glass in salute, and then took a healthy sip before speaking. "Kaili is prepared to stay with you."

I sipped the amber liquid, relishing the smooth burn as it slid down my throat. "Something you don't condone?"

We sat on the winged-back chairs that overlooked the gardens. They were beautiful at night, lit with a string of lanterns that looked like diamonds amid the darkness.

"Would it matter?"

"I respect you. If you honestly believe I'm not suited for your daughter, I will take my leave of her."

That induced a laugh from him, something I didn't expect.

"I appreciate that, Zebastian, but this also involves Kaili. She will be most difficult to live with should I deny your union."

"What would ease your heart?"

"I would ask you to wait another year."

Not an intolerable request. Why did it make my heart feel heavy? "May I ask why?"

He took another swig of his drink, casting his gaze to the window. "She's not had much time to ... think about this."

A low growl rose from my chest. "You want her to see other males?"

He scoffed. "Do you really think she could?"

"I do not."

"Arcadie has offered to train you to control your rage and ability to reap."

The brandy in my mouth remained there, my throat too tight to swallow. To be trained by an elder of such standing is an honor not freely given. Eager to accept the offer, I forced the liquid down. Brandy burns if eased down too narrow a passage. I coughed and spewed like a whelp taking his first drink.

Khalen stood and poured me a glass of water as I

continued to hack without grace. I drank the cool liquid, feeling like a dolt.

"Arcadie helped train me when I was a lad. He's very good."

I nodded, still unable to speak.

"You will need to move to Brazil, of course."

"And Kaili?" I rasped out, my throat still raw from the burn.

"Will remain home."

"Does she know this?"

"I thought the news would be best delivered by you."

"Best for who?" She would not take the news lightly. Giving up on the drink, I placed the glass down on the table.

"You could see each other often. Ian makes the trip frequently with his mate, Erika."

"Very well. I will inform Kaili tonight."

Khalen downed the rest of his drink. "You make a fine addition to our clan, Zebastian. We are blessed to have you."

Would my father think the same?

MY FATHER STOOD FROM THE dinner table, clinking his glass with a fork until all conversations ceased.

"I have an announcement to make."

Kaili squeezed my hand under the table, apprehension laced in her eyes.

"As you all know, my son, Zebastian, has returned to our clan. His skills and bravery have restored my pride." His gray eyes fixed on me, though it wasn't pride making them shine. "As a result, Hiren has agreed to bless him with his fine daughter, Tishana, to be his mate."

A roar of pleasure rose from the crowd. Kaili's hand

fell from mine.

I stood, knocking my chair to the ground. The loud thud demanded attention. "Though the gift is a generous one," I stated. "I have already chosen a mate." I looked down at Kaili, reaching for her hand so she would stand beside me. She did so with hesitation.

Murmurs rumbled through the air like insects feasting on ripe crop.

"Impossible union," said Father. "Kaili, though fine in blood and breeding, is not a shifter."

"Yet, my choice is made."

We locked eyes for what seemed like minutes before he pushed his chair back. Tossing his napkin aside, he strode toward me.

"Do I take this as a challenge, Zebastian?"

"I do not falter from my decision."

"Outside," he growled. "We end this at once."

Releasing Kaili's hand, I followed him out. She ran to catch up.

"You cannot challenge him."

"I must, or forever be in his shadow."

"You finally got your family back, Ze. Don't make me the cause of their loss."

I stopped, turning her to face me. "You are worth the world to me. Never forget that. If my father cannot accept my choices, that is his issue, not yours—never yours."

Teak ran to catch up to us. "What are you doing?"

"What I must."

"The man will make mincemeat of you."

"Thanks for the support, Teak."

"And what of your rage? Have you thought about that?"

"More than a few times, my friend. Keep Kaili safe for

me, yes?"

Outside, the crowd gathered around, leaving me and my father in the midst of their circle. Challenges were common in shifter societies. They were the backbone of hierarchy, the reason leaders ruled with authority and confidence. If I won, I earned the right to oust my father and take his place. If I lost, my father ruled my future or took my life. I could deny the challenge and simply leave with Khalen come morning, but doing so would shame my father and his clan. I would be labeled deserter and coward. This was not a legend I would strap to my mate and children for any reason. Khalen knew this as well, which is why he didn't voice up.

Kaili tried pleading with him, but he shook his head, attempting to explain his reasons. He was a leader and knew the importance and certainty of a challenge. He would not interfere.

Ren entered the circle. Being the elder of the clan, he made the rules of this challenge and was the one to enforce them should things get out of hand.

"Tiban, do you accept this challenge?"

Raising his chin up and widening his stance, he said, "I do."

"Zebastian, son of Tiban, do you accept this challenge?"

"I do." The thought of fighting my father regressed me back to my childhood, making me feel vulnerable and weak. I was raised to be respectful—everything this was not. Could I hurt him if necessary? More the question ... could I control my rage? If not, this would end badly for everyone. Killing was not permitted in a challenge unless he won and I refused to yield to his demands.

"Use of gifts is not permitted," said Ren. "You fight as humans, not animals. The fight ends when someone submits by tapping out, or I deem it so. Any questions?"

"None," said Father.

I, too, stated, "None."

Ren pressed himself back into the circle of bystanders. "Begin."

I never considered myself a skilled fighter. My wolf held its own in battle, but I never had much cause for human hand-to-hand. My chances of winning this challenge were slim at best, and I knew it. Teak was right. At my father's hand, I would become mincemeat.

He circled me, sizing me up for a lesson he longed to issue since my return. Fueled by the vengeful memory of my brother's death, my father harnessed a distinct advantage. I didn't have time to tell him the truth of things, nor did I think he would listen. Perhaps when this battle ended, we would have words, provided I survived. Yielding to his command was not my intention—win or lose.

His first blow came fast and hard, connecting to my jaw. I blocked the next blow and countered with a jab to his stomach. He didn't flinch. Two uppercuts to my chin and a hook to my temple sent my mind reeling. I stumbled back.

Gabrihen caught me by the shoulders. "Use his momentum against him. Get out of the way."

When Father came flying at me feet first, I did as Gabrihen suggested. Shifting left, Father's foot flew past. I grabbed it and slung him to the ground, knocking the wind from his lungs.

When he recovered, he came at me with a hard jab to my stomach. I hunched back, blocked the blow with crossed arms, and then twisted his arm into a painful joint lock, something Gabrihen used on me during one of our many skirmishes. What I didn't predict was the use of Father's feet. He jumped up, twisted around, aiming his heel at my knee. I went down like a house of cards in a windstorm.

His entire weight came upon me as his fist found my face. Blood seeped from my torn lip and loosened teeth. I tried twisting away, but his body didn't yield. My rage hovered on the surface, making it difficult to think.

"Do it," he growled. "Show them all the demon within—the demon that killed Carter."

"No!" I tossed him away and scrambled to my feet. He came at me with renewed vengeance. "I didn't kill him."

When he tried to grab me, I tossed him to the ground, feeling stronger than I ever remembered. My rage had found a new avenue. Fear shone in his eyes as I held him firm beneath me with pure strength and determination.

"I saw you with his blood on your maw."

"I was trying to save him. The blood you saw was that of the guard who killed Carter."

When he fought to get free, my grip tightened. We remained that way for several minutes. His face darkened, his breathing labored. He was weakening. I, on the other hand, felt strength in search of an outlet. My grip became tighter.

"Ahg," he yelled.

"Do you yield?"

"No."

He would never yield to me, no matter how much pain I inflicted. The man was strong and plagued with pride that would see him to his grave before ever surrendering.

More time passed as he grew weaker.

"Done!" Ren announced. "Zebastian wins."

I released my father. He roared with resentment.

Ren stood between us, and then looked to me. "Name your demands."

"I choose to return with Khalen and take his daughter as mate. I leave this clan in the capable hands of my father to resume his rule as before."

"Done," said Ren.

The crowd chatted in wild chaos. My desires were no secret and should not have come as a surprise, yet there were some members clearly perplexed. My mother came to comfort Father. He shrugged her away—something I felt compelled to address.

"Give us a moment," I asked her.

"Of course." She strode away with the others.

"Have you not done enough to shame me?" asked Father.

"Now that you know the truth of things, it's time to move on. Release this anger or lose what you once loved forever. I love you and will always be your son. You have to make the choice to be my father and to be the mate Mother deserves. This pride of yours will destroy you. Can you not see her pain?"

He stood in silence, his clear gray eyes searching the depths of my own. Pools of tears threatened to fall as he sank to his knees and looked up at the dark cloud-filled sky. "I miss him, Zebastian. Not a day goes by when his face isn't in my memories."

I knelt beside him. "We all miss him, Father. I'm sorry I couldn't save him. If I had been faster to react I ..."

"No," he said, placing his strong hand on my shoulder. "Do not carry this blame any further. You are right. This anger has clouded my judgment, has made me bitter and cold. You've made the right decision to leave with Khalen, a man more deserving of your respect."

Standing, I reached down to help him stand. "I respect you as much."

With hesitation, he accepted the help. "When do you intend to join with Kaili?"

"I promised Khalen I'd wait a year while Arcadie trains me to harness my rage and skill of reaping."

"Arcadie?"

"Yes. The offer surprised me as well."

He slapped my shoulder, making me wince. "You've done well for yourself, my son." He looked toward the commons building where Mother stood waiting. "I have some mending to do it seems."

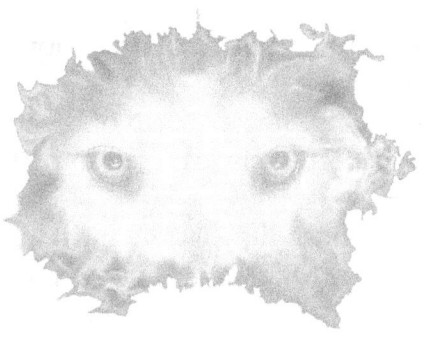

Chapter 33

-Zebastian-

"BRAZIL?" KAILI SAT UP IN bed, her green eyes wide as the moon.

"Just for a year, love. Khalen said you can visit often."

"A whole year?"

"It will go by quickly." I urged her to lay by my side, so I could stroke her soft skin. "Come now. I want to love you through the night and embed my scent upon you."

Giving in to my touch and kisses, she sank down beside me. "I don't want to sleep."

"Sleeping is not what I have in mind."

As **WE PACKED THE PLANE** and prepared to leave. Father approached me, his arm wrapped protectively around my mother. The glow in her face and the warmth in her smile said more than words could muster.

Father placed a pendant in my hand, closing my fingers around it. "Place that around your mate, my son, and welcome her into the family."

"We expect to see you at the ceremony."

"Of course."

Kaili came over and gave each of them a hug. Leaning into my father's ear, she whispered something that made him smile.

I took the pendant he gave me and lowered the leather loop over Kaili's head. "With this pendant, I claim you, Kaili Dunning, as my own, to be joined with my soul in one year's time."

She lifted the yellow stone and placed a kiss upon it. "This will be a long year."

"What did you whisper to Father that has him smiling so?"

"I promised him many grandchildren."

The thought of it warmed my soul. "Did you now?"

"Providing I survive this year so far from your side."

I kissed her long and hard. "I'll make sure you do, my angel."

"Promise?"

"You have my word."

- The End -

A Note From the Author

I hope you have enjoyed reading Shifter. This one was a hard one for me to write seeing I share many of the trials that Ze and Kaili had to face. This story went through many revisions and two complete rewrites. Letting it go is like saying goodbye to an old friend. Odd thing to think, I know, but that is how it feels. Writers tend to get caught up in the stories they weave, and I am no exception.

Ze is an amazing character. He will appear again within the saga, I'm sure. With training, he will realize his full potential. When that happens, watch out. He'll be as strong, if not stronger, than Khalen.

About the Author

Rowena started writing at a young age, feeling an inherent need to tell stories that inspire and reflect aspects of life that are rarely considered.

Being a descendant of James Hudson Taylor, author and founder of the China Inland Mission, Rowena comes from a long line of storytellers, including her mother and father. The tradition of writing continues through her daughter, Erika.

Rowena's goal is to inspire others to tell their stories and share the wonderful gift and adventure of life. She often speaks before groups, sharing her experiences of writing and telling stories. It is a passion of hers that she shares with her mate, Gregg.

Though she is over ninety percent blind, Rowena doesn't allow that to derail her ambitions. Her husband is deaf, so they make the perfect pair. They live on the Olympic Peninsula in Washington with her guide dog Skye-Bear.

Other Books by Rowena

Protected
Union
Legend
Aeon Pneuma
Illusions
Fealty
Shifter

SHORT STORIES
Aeneas

www.RowenaPortch.com